MAGICKEEPERS

THE ETERNAL HOURGLASS
BOOK ONE

ERICA KIROV

Jabberwocky
SOURCEBOOKS
AN IMPRINT OF SOURCEBOOKS

Published by Sourcebooks Jabberwocky, an imprint of Sourcebooks, Inc.
P.O. Box 4410, Naperville, Illinois 60567–4410
(630) 961–3900
Fax: (630) 961–2168
www.jabberwockykids.com

Library of Congress Cataloging-in-Publication Data

Kirov, Erica.
  Magickeepers : the eternal hourglass / by Erica Kirov.
      p. cm.
  Summary: Living in Las Vegas with his unsuccessful father, Nick Rostov learns on his thirteenth birthday that he is descended from a powerful line of Russian Magickeepers on his dead mother's side, and that the equally powerful but evil Shadowkeepers will stop at nothing to get an ancient relic that his grandfather gave him.
  [1. Magic—Fiction. 2. Magicians—Fiction. 3. Good and evil—Fiction. 4. Family—Fiction. 5. Russia—History—Fiction. 6. Las Vegas (Nev.)—Fiction.] I. Title. II. Title: Eternal hourglass.
  PZ7.K6382Mag 2009
  [Fic]—dc22

                             2008047718

                Printed and bound in the United States of America.
                    LB 10 9 8 7 6 5 4 3 2 1

To my father, for instilling in me a pride in my Russian heritage.
To my mother, for teaching me to live in the moment.
And to my children, Alexa, Nicholas, Isabella, and Jack,
for teaching me what it means to love.

ACKNOWLEDGMENTS

A huge thank you, as always, to my agent, Jay Poynor, who was enchanted by the book idea, and who has never failed to support me in my writing endeavors.

To Lyron Bennett, my editor at Jabberwocky, who drove the writing of this book—his notes, his questions…I met my match as a writer. I appreciate all the inspiration and ideas he offered. The book—and I as a writer—gained infinitely from his insights.

To Irina Polyakova, who translated phrases into Russian for me and was more than generous with her knowledge of linguistics and Russian culture. I very much appreciate her patience with me.

To Writer's Cramp—Pam, Jon, and Melody—for Tuesdays and the power of conference calls, friendship, dedication, and…sushi.

To my young friends—the "gang" at New Hope—Miranda, Lauren, Allison, Maggie, Josh, and most especially Jacob, who always makes me feel like a special author.

To my nieces and nephews, whom I adore: Tyler, Zachary, and Tori and Cassidy (Twins #1); and Pannos and his sisters, Sofia and Evanthia (Twins #2).

And finally, to my own family. Most especially, for this book, to my children, who have so wonderfully understood deadlines, and helped me name tigers and polar bears and envision a world in which magic exists. Because in the end, family is magic.

The power of thought—the magic of the mind!
—Lord Byron

The magic of the tongue is the most dangerous of all spells.
—Edward Bulwer-Lytton

My brain is the key that sets my mind free.
—Harry Houdini

CONTENTS

PROLOGUE

Princess Theatre, Montreal, Canada, 1926

THE MYSTERIOUS MAN IN THE BLACK WOOL CLOAK SAT in the front row of the Princess Theatre, precisely in the center seat. He set his top hat on his knees, and his rough beard straggled down, like a bird's nest after a storm. The man waited for the finale of the show, speaking to no one, not even his companion. Instead, he stared intently with pale, magnetic eyes as the most famous magician in the world, Harry Houdini, announced his next trick from the stage.

"Ladies and gentlemen, introducing my original invention, the Water Torture Cell."

As the audience hushed, Houdini, short and muscular with a head of dark hair and wearing a simple black bathing suit, was draped in chains by his wife, Bess. A policeman from the audience was brought onstage wearing a dapper uniform, badge gleaming under the spotlights. Holding up his own handcuffs, the policeman pulled Houdini's arms behind his back and clapped the cuffs on tightly, checking them several times before nodding. The chains wrapped around Houdini's body were heavy and clinked and rattled with every move he made. Finally, two huge padlocks were attached to the chains and locked dramatically with shining brass keys.

Slowly, the magician was lifted—upside down—and suspended over the glass torture chamber filled to the top with ice-cold water. Bess signaled, and Houdini was lowered until his head almost touched the beckoning water.

Bess told the crowd, "Take one last breath with the master, Houdini, and see how long you can hold it."

The crowd inhaled as one. Houdini filled his lungs with air—*one last breath*—and was lowered into the water, first his head, neck, then body, and finally his feet, before Bess fastened the top. The chamber was not big enough for Houdini to turn around in. A thick curtain was drawn. An hourglass was overturned.

"He must emerge before this sand runs out," Bess announced to the crowd. "Or he will drown."

Not one whisper could be heard in the theater. Patrons in fur coats and fancy theater dress leaned forward, women in plumage and jewels knotted their hands together anxiously. The man in the cloak heard people exhaling around him as they gasped for breath. He watched the sands trickling, as if he were somehow counting each grain. Now, as the sands ran down inside the hourglass, members of the audience murmured. Someone near the man in the cloak whispered, "It's impossible to hold your breath that long. They must free him."

"It's been two minutes!" Bess exclaimed from the stage, panic in her voice. "He cannot survive."

Bess parted the curtain, revealing Houdini struggling wildly with his shackles. Frantically, she closed the curtain and ran for the safety ax, ready to smash the glass and free her beloved husband from the throes of death. She raised the ax as the audience gasped in horror.

The man in the cloak saw those around him frozen at the edge of their seats as if statues. Seconds passed. The curtain rose.

The Water Torture Cell was empty.

At that moment, a dripping wet and smiling Houdini was revealed, standing atop the torture cell, arms raised above his head in triumph.

The crowd in the Princess Theatre rose to their feet as if they were one, stamping and clapping their approval, whistles and shouts of "Bravo!" ringing through the theater. But not the man in the cloak with the icy eyes. He stared, not at Houdini, but at the hourglass that had sifted the sparkling sand. He could see the lettering etched along its gold-rimmed top.

His companion leaned close to him and whispered in his ear, "Is that it, Master?"

The man in the cloak nodded, his eyes narrow with fury. "Yes."

"Now what?"

"We must do whatever it takes."

Eight days later, Harry Houdini, revered showman, the most famous magician ever to have lived, was dead.

A LESS-THAN-STELLAR
BIRTHDAY REPORT CARD

*N*ICK ROSTOV STARED DOWN AT HIS END-OF-YEAR REPORT
card.

One F. Two Cs. One B-minus. And an A. In Health.

He tried to imagine how he would explain to his dad that
his lone A was for the class that taught where babies came
from; that he knew what a fallopian tube was, but square
roots eluded him.

If he thought his report card was bad, lunch was a disaster.
When he walked into the cafeteria, an overwhelming stench
overpowered him—way worse than Tuna-Surprise Tuesdays
and Mystery-Meat Mondays. The usual lady in the hairnet
had been replaced by a creepy guy with long, wiry hair and
strange eyes, and whatever the guy was serving didn't look
good—and smelled worse. The smell was so gross that Nick

didn't eat and instead fished from his backpack a pulverized snack-size bag of potato chips, which had been crushed into smithereens by his math book. This meant he actually ate potato chip *dust,* and his stomach growled all afternoon.

When the final bell rang, he grabbed his skateboard from his locker and waved good-bye to a couple of kids in the hall. Once he was off school property, Nick rode his board down the hot Nevada sidewalk in the general direction of the hotel where he lived in a suite with his dad.

He'd attended two schools in the last three years. Every time his dad was fired or changed jobs, they moved. Nick bent his knees and jumped a curb on his skateboard.

Living in hotels with his dad meant whenever Nick made a friend at the hotel pool, the kid was on vacation. He figured over the last three or four years, he'd made a hundred friends, and not one of them lived in Las Vegas. He once had a friend from Belize. He didn't even know where Belize was.

Nick rode his skateboard into a big parking lot by the high school, the wheels making a steady *whish-whish* noise. He didn't want to go home—not with that report card. Not that his dad would say much, but he always had a sad look on his face. Bad report cards only made it sadder.

Nick didn't know how long he rode his skateboard, hopping curbs, jumping over banged-up trash cans lying on their sides. The last two cars left the high school's parking lot, two

2

teachers with bulging briefcases, grinning from ear to ear. Even teachers were happy when school let out for summer.

Finally, he started toward home, the sky clear and cloudless. When he arrived at the Pendragon Hotel and Casino, the doorman, Jack, asked him, "How'd you do on your report card?"

"Don't ask."

"That good, huh?"

"Yeah."

"Then you may not want to go up. Your grandfather is here. Louisa in housekeeping called me. You can hear them yelling all the way down the hallway."

"Great. Just what I need. Dad will be in an even worse mood."

Nick sighed, picked up his board, walked through the lobby, and rode up in the elevator—the one with the light that sometimes flickered like a horror movie. He stepped off when it arrived at his floor. Out of the corner of his eye, he thought he saw something move. He whirled around in time to see a weird shadow on the wall. He took a few steps toward that end of the hall, and the shadow slid under a room door. Nick didn't see a single thing that could have created the shadow.

"What the…?" Shadows didn't appear from nothing. Nick hesitated but walked closer to the door where it had disappeared.

The closer he got, the more he smelled…well, he didn't know what it was. But it was worse than his gym locker after not washing his P.E. uniform all year. It reminded him of the cafeteria's strange odor at lunch. Could a lunchroom stench follow you home? Or was it something weirder than that?

Nick shivered. Whatever had gone under that door—shadow and stench—he didn't want to be near it. So he ran down the hall as fast as he could, looking over his shoulder every couple of strides. When he reached his door, he could hear his father and grandfather arguing.

"I told you, Gus, absolutely not!" his father's voice was loud. His dad never yelled. He gave Nick that "I'm disappointed in you, son" speech, but he never yelled, not even at Grandpa.

"It doesn't matter if you refuse. It's in his bloodline."

"Don't talk to me about this. The answer is no."

"*She* would have wanted him to go. She would have wanted to know. For sure. Once and for all. I know my daughter. She would have."

"She wouldn't. That's why we're even here, Gus. She was hiding from them. From her past."

"You're a fool! Sooner or later, he'll find out for himself. You can't fight it."

Nick's heart pounded. He leaned his ear closer to the door. *Find out what?*

Down the hall, he thought he saw something move.

Regardless of the fight on the other side of the door, Nick would rather be in there with his dad and grandfather yelling at each other, than out in the hall where things were getting creepier by the second. He slipped his card key in the lock and opened the door.

"Nick, my boy," his grandfather turned around, a big smile on his face, acting as though nothing had happened. "I was just leaving. But I'll see you for your birthday tomorrow. A teenager! I can't believe it…thirteen. You make me feel older than I already am."

His grandfather grabbed Nick in a bear hug. Nick looked over at his dad, who was glaring at them.

After his grandfather left, Nick asked, "What were you two arguing about?"

"We weren't arguing."

"I heard you. You're always arguing lately."

His father shook his head. "Your grandfather has his own ideas about how you should be raised. And I have mine."

"I wish you two would get along."

"Sometimes there are some things so important that people just can't agree. Anyway, don't worry about it, okay?" He glanced at his watch. "I need to get ready."

His dad went to his bedroom to change into his tuxedo. He performed every night, twice on Saturday, as the magician at the Pendragon. He sawed an assistant in half, and he could pull a white dove out of his hat. But Nick knew he was really, really bad at it. He also told horrible jokes. His father thought they were really funny—but Nick had been in the audience. People actually groaned.

His dad returned to the living room, looking dapper in his slightly thread-worn black tuxedo. He asked, "If Houdini were alive today, what would he be doing?"

"Dad, I've heard this joke before. I've heard it like fifty times before."

"Humor me. What would he be doing?"

"Scratching on the inside of his coffin."

His father started laughing. "That one always cracks me up."

Nick just shook his head.

His dad walked to the door to leave.

"Oh, Dad, before you go out in the hall, there was a really weird smell out there earlier."

"Like what?"

"I don't know, but...it was down at the other end of the hall."

His father opened the door and sniffed the air. "I don't smell anything. Maybe it was room service." He laughed at his own joke. "All right, buddy, there's a microwavable TV dinner in the freezer. Or you can have room service make you something—if you dare. Have a good night, okay?"

Nick nodded. After his dad left, Nick poked his head out in the hall. Whatever that odor was, it was gone.

He shut the door and smiled to himself. He hated when his grandfather and dad fought. But there was one good thing that came from it.

His dad had forgotten to ask for his report card.

A GIFT, THE GIFT

THE NEXT NIGHT—HIS BIRTHDAY—NICK STOOD INSIDE THE red-velvet and tarnished-gold lobby of the Pendragon Hotel and Casino, hands in his pockets, waiting for his grandfather. Finally, Nick spied him walking across the lobby's worn carpeting, a big smile on his face.

"Waiting long, birthday boy?" he asked Nick, giving him a hug.

"No. Where are we going to eat? I'm *starving*." In fact, he thought he might just die if he didn't get a cheeseburger soon.

"You're always starving. I don't know where you put it all. Anyway, I can't tell you where we're going. It's a surprise. But we're already late." He practically dragged Nick along as they hurried out of the casino and climbed into Grandpa's car.

Grandpa drove the biggest purple Cadillac convertible in Las Vegas, complete with fuzzy purple dice hanging from the rearview mirror. Nick supposed that it was the biggest purple Cadillac in the world, actually, as he didn't imagine there were many people willing to drive around in something so unbelievably, horrifically embarrassing.

"And where did you say we were going?" Nick asked as they pulled away and snaked through the streets of Las Vegas.

"Do you honestly think I'm going to fall for that? Can't trick me. I'm not that old. A surprise, I told you," Grandpa said, his white handlebar mustache wiggling with pent-up amusement.

Nick stared up at the neon lights of the city. Bulbs danced in synchronized staccato, advertising casinos, hotels, and Las Vegas's most spectacular shows—including the most famous of them all, the magician Damian. Tickets were sold out three years in advance, and they were so expensive that Nick figured there was no chance he'd ever see the show, much as he wanted to.

A steamy June breeze ruffled his hair—which his father was always nagging him to cut—as they left the city. They were headed into the desert. Nick stared out at the expanse of nothingness, just dust and sand and highway. He looked at himself in the side-view mirror. He was tall for his age and thin, with dark brown, wavy hair that hit the collar of his shirt. He had freckles scattered across the bridge of his nose, leading, like a crooked path, to his pale blue eyes. Those eyes were the same color as Grandpa's, which were the same color as Nick's mother's, who died when Nick was a baby.

Grandpa drove on and on in the desert until Las Vegas was nothing more than a glowing speck far behind them. Nick stared up at the sky, which was blanketed with stars. The farther they drove, the smaller and more alone Nick felt—even though Grandpa was right beside him. Eventually, they reached a side road and turned left. There was no sign.

"Are you sure you know where you're going?"

"Absolutely, Nicky," Grandpa replied. His round belly, which resembled a department store Santa's, nearly touched the steering wheel.

Up ahead, a wooden house stood lonely beneath a hollow moon. When they drove closer, he realized it was actually a store of some sort. Grandpa pulled up in front of it.

"Here we are," Grandpa said as he put the car in park and looked over at Nick. "Come on, then. We're late."

Nick peered through the windshield at the sign on the door.

"Madame Bogdonovich's Magical Curiosity Shoppe?"

"She's expecting us."

Nick clambered out of Grandpa's purple monstrosity and walked up the steps, Grandpa behind him.

"How the heck would anyone find this place if they wanted to buy something? This has to be the *least* successful magic shop ever."

Nick peered in the window, but all he saw were shadows. He loved learning magic tricks, but his father hated it. Even though his dad was a magician, he always said he wanted Nick to become something—anything—else.

Grandpa reached the top step, and Nick opened the door. A bell gently chimed.

"Just *von* minute!" a high voice, almost like an opera singer's, sang out to them.

From behind a curtain that jangled with beads, an old woman emerged with makeup decorating her eyes that made them look like two butterfly wings and a deep purple and green scarf around her wild, gray, curly hair. Gold bracelets clinked, crowding her arms from her wrists to her elbows. She wore a long, green velvet ball gown and what looked like an enormous emerald necklace that seemed to glow.

"Gustav!" she purred at Nick's grandfather. "You've brought him!"

He nodded. "Nick, allow me to present Madame B."

"Hi!" Nick lifted his hand in an awkward wave. He looked around the shop, which was mind-bogglingly crowded, a jumble of colorful scarves, hoops and rings, satin boxes, books on magic, top hats, wands, costumes, capes, and mannequins.

Crystal balls competed with mason jars that had labels handwritten in a spidery script: bat liver, ground Siberian caribou antler, condensed whale milk. Nick tried to avoid staring.

"Come!" Madame B. commanded. She glanced over her shoulder at Nick's grandfather. "He's *handsome,* with those *eyes* just like his mama." Looking back at Nick, she said, "Happy birthday, my darling."

"Thanks." Nick tried to look over his own shoulder at Grandpa. He wanted to ask, *Who is this crazy person?* But he was quickly whisked behind a dark curtain and half-pushed into a huge velvet chair. Nick felt as though he had sunk almost to the floor.

Grandpa ducked through the curtain, too. He and Madame B. sat on the other side of a small, round table covered with a blood red satin, tablecloth. Grandpa's and Madame B.'s chairs weren't quite as squishy as Nick's so they seemed to sit up much higher than he did, peering down at him like a specimen under a microscope. Nick squirmed.

Madame B. reached into a large, black leather bag and pulled out a crystal ball the size of an ostrich egg. She set it on a brass pedestal engraved with hieroglyphics.

"Look," Madame B. commanded, drawing out the word with an exotic accent when she spoke. She tapped a long, red-varnished nail against the crystal ball. "Tell us *vhat* you see."

"Well, I can't…" sputtered Nick, thinking this had to be the strangest birthday ever, which, considering he was with Grandpa, was saying a lot. "I don't know how—"

"Shh!" the old woman hissed. "You *can*. Look. Loooook!"

Nick stared meaningfully at Grandpa. They had to be kidding him. His father always said, in a town full of showgirls and oddballs, some of them were out of "central casting"— meaning Madame B. probably thought she was in a movie. But more likely, she was just crazy.

"Try, Nick," Grandpa urged. "For me."

Sighing and fidgeting in his seat, Nick rolled his eyes, then leaned forward as best he could in the chair to stare at the crystal ball. All he saw was his own face reflected back, distorted, while Grandpa and the crazy magic-shop owner seemed to look back at him with pin-dot heads showing through the other side, as if he was watching them through funhouse glass.

"I don't see anything. There, you happy?" He flopped back in his chair.

"Noooooooooooooo," the old woman batted her long caterpillar-like lashes. She looked at Grandpa and snapped, "Gustav, I hope you are right about this one."

"Trust me," he said.

Nick exhaled loudly. He hated when grown-ups talked about him when he was right there. "Right about what?"

"Look," Madame B. said. "You must breathe deeply, like this." She took a big breath. "Then, you look with your *mind*, not your eyes. Easy." She snapped her fingers. "I used to gaze in it for the Tsarina. *Eet's* a good ball. Try."

Feeling hungry—and frustrated—Nick tried again. He took a deep breath and peered into the crystal ball. He tried not to focus on how ridiculous his face was reflected in it, but instead gazed inside his mind, kind of like daydreaming— which his teachers always complained he was exceedingly good at doing during class.

Suddenly, Nick saw a flash. He jumped, quickly moving his head from left to right as if to shake the images from his mind.

"He can see!" Madame B. whispered loudly. "Tell us, my *leetle* one. Tell us."

Nick blinked hard several times. The crystal ball was foggy now, but he could make out a scene. His temples pounded, and for a minute, he thought he might throw up. The room felt hot. "I see..." He squinted. "I see a desert. It must be Las Vegas."

"Never assume, *zaychik*," the old woman warned.

"Sand. Lots of sand. It has to be Vegas. And there's...the sphinx. It's Vegas. The Luxor Hotel."

"Do you see neon?" Grandpa asked.

"Hmm, funny." Nick looked hard. "I don't. Wait...there's a pyramid. And camels."

Grandpa leaned forward. "Go ahead, Nick, what else?"

"And...and there's a man, in robes. And around him are men with swords."

Grandpa slapped Madame B. on the arm. "I told you!" he beamed.

"He's...there are birds around him. The men are cutting the birds' heads off with swords." He pressed forward, his nose almost touching the ball. "And he's making them come alive again. The man in the robes. It's a trick—an illusion. He's a magician!"

Nick's head ached, and he fell back against the chair feeling strangely tired. The crystal ball looked like a regular glass ball again. "What happened?"

"A *vonderful* thing," Madame B. smiled at him. "A most miraculous thing. Our world has been waiting for you, child. You, Nicholai Rostov, have the *gift*."

THE ALL·YOU·CAN·
ASK BUFFET

WHAT HAPPENED IN THERE, GRANDPA?" NICK ASKED OVER
supper. Grandpa liked to go to all-you-can-eat buffets on
the Las Vegas Strip. The idea, according to Grandpa, was to eat
so much you couldn't move—to make sure you got your money's
worth. He always insisted they start with the most expensive
stuff—shrimp and crab legs—before even considering "moving
down the food chain" to things like salad and potatoes.

Nick lifted a french fry drowning in ketchup to his mouth.
"What kind of trick was it? How did she do that with the
crystal ball?"

Nick knew how to do all of his dad's tricks. He could make
a ball disappear and pull a coin out from someone's ear. He
could make the ace of hearts jump out from the middle of a
deck of cards. He knew how most magicians did levitations

and the disappearing-woman-in-the-box trick. But the crystal ball—*that* was cool.

"She didn't do anything, Nick. You did."

Nick looked across the table at his grandfather. Nick's father said that Grandpa was an eccentric in a town full of eccentrics. When Nick was younger, he asked his father what that meant. Basically, Nick found out that *eccentric* was a grown-up's way of saying someone was a little crazy. "But in a good way," his father had said.

"So is this like the time you told me the moon was following us?" Nick folded his arms. "Or the time you told me that Damian's show is real magic?"

"Yes and no."

"A grown-up's way of saying he told a lie." Nick rolled his eyes.

"No. The moon didn't really follow us. That's an optical illusion. But yes," Grandpa lowered his voice to a whisper, "Damian's show is real. Nick, when he fights the swordsmen in his show and plunges a knife in a woman's heart and turns her into a dove to free her from the prison, it's *real*. No one has ever, in the history of magic, done what he can do. He is real. He's of the purest magic line. And yes, you really could see the past in that crystal ball. Back to the time of the Pharaohs. You did it, Nick."

"Sure."

"Your mother could, too."

Nick exhaled, and his heart skipped a beat. "My mother?" He had no real memory of her, but her photos were all around the suite at the Pendragon. In each framed picture, Nick's mother was dressed in her magician's assistant costumes— ruby red sequins and feathers, her pale eyes sparkling with rhinestones on the ends of her long false eyelashes. Back then, Nick's father had been a successful magician. His tricks had always worked. Dad called his mother his good luck charm, and after she died, he told Nick that his tricks had broken, just like his heart. When Nick thought about his mom, his throat sometimes hurt.

"Your mother had the gift. You're like her, Nicholai. Magic is real. Its roots go back to Egypt."

"The pyramids I saw."

His grandfather nodded. "It's a bloodline, Nick. Wait until we're outside to talk about this more," he said, looking around the room. "The walls have ears."

"What does that mean?"

"It means I can't say anything more until we get outside."

Actually, Nick thought, it meant Grandpa was, just as his father said, crazy in a good way.

Grandpa left a tip on the table and stood to leave.

"I can't move." Nick rubbed his stomach. "Think it'll help me gain a few pounds?" He was tired of his jeans always sagging—and not in a cool way, but in a thin, dorky, few-pizzas-short-of-a-real-waist way.

"Nick," Grandpa sighed, "I wish I had your problem, kiddo."

"I still can't move."

"We have to. Come on. I've got to get you back to your father."

Once they left the restaurant, they walked to the Pendragon, three blocks away. In front of them, down the street, Las Vegas rose like a neon Oz.

"Tell me more about magic. About what I saw in the crystal ball." It wasn't that he believed his grandfather's crazy claims—but the crystal ball had seemed so real.

"Magic goes back to Egypt. But then magicians were persecuted and they scattered across the globe. There's much about magic that's both secret and true." His grandfather slung an arm around Nick's shoulders. "Too much for me to tell you about tonight. But I want you to be very careful, Nick."

"Of what?"

"Magic can be dangerous when it falls into the wrong hands." He looked over his shoulder and then whispered, "Into *enemy* hands. For now, we'll keep your gift a secret. Okay?"

"Sure." As if he would even know how to tell someone about the crystal ball. Besides, he lived in a hotel, not a neighborhood, and didn't have that many friends to tell. They strolled up to the Pendragon and stood beneath its neon dragon sign. Penny, as Nick called the dragon, breathed fire when the machine worked, but most of the time, it didn't.

"Are you going to come up, Grandpa?"

He shook his head. "I think not. You know how he can be."

Nick nodded.

Grandpa pressed something into the palm of Nick's hand. "It's your birthday gift. Open it when you're alone. It belonged to your mother."

Nick looked down at the small wrapped box. "Thanks, Grandpa."

He hugged his grandfather good-bye and entered the Pendragon, which stood in the old part of Las Vegas, not the shiny, new, glamorously tacky part. The Pendragon didn't have a roller coaster in its lobby, or a pirate ship complete with pirates. No dancing fountains greeted guests as they arrived. No gondolas floated on an indoor Venetian canal. It didn't have one of the shows people booked years in advance to see, like the magician Damian. It didn't even have much neon. The slot machines in the Pendragon were old, and the burgundy carpeting in the casino and the hallways was worn. Even the showgirls were old by showgirl standards. "Beats retiring," Margot, the star of the show, once told Nick.

He shuffled toward the elevators and heard guests muttering in the lobby.

"Worst magic act I've ever seen."

"I could do that trick."

"He's no Damian, that's for sure."

Nick sighed, shoved the gift deep into his jeans pocket, and took the elevator up to the thirteenth floor. He walked down the hall and opened the door. Posters of famous magicians like Houdini, Carter, and Blackstone hung on the walls next to framed glossy photos of his parents from when their magic act was a hit.

"Dad?" he called out.

"One minute," his dad replied from the kitchen. He emerged a brief time later, holding a cake with glowing candles in front of him. "Happy birthday…" he sang.

"Please don't sing."

"You have to sing on your birthday. And make a wish."

"Please," Nick begged him.

But his dad barreled on through the song, off-key and really loud. When he finished, Nick shut his eyes and blew out the candles.

"Did you make a wish?" Dad was still wearing his tuxedo from the show, but with the bow tie undone.

"Sure," Nick said, but he hadn't. Wishes were for babies.

Dad put the cake on the counter separating the galley kitchen—just a half-sized refrigerator and a tiny stove and a microwave—from their even smaller living room. "Want a piece? The chef made it special for you."

Nick looked at the lopsided cake with the red-hued icing. It had "Happy Birthday, Nicholai" on it, but the chef had clearly run out of room, so the last three letters actually dropped over the side of the cake. Besides having the worst magic act in Las Vegas, the Pendragon, Nick knew, was equally infamous for its terrible food.

"I'm actually so stuffed I feel gross."

"Grandpa took you to one of those all-you-can-eat places again, didn't he?"

Nick nodded.

"Still trying to get his money's worth?"

Nick laughed. "Yeah. I think he really did get his money's worth tonight. He ate four linebacker-sized plates of oysters and shrimp. I had three cheeseburgers. And a plate of fries. Oh, and a lobster tail."

"Only in Vegas can you get that combination."

Nick grinned sheepishly. "So if you don't mind, I think I'll save my cake for breakfast tomorrow."

"Sure, Kolya," his father said, calling him by the Russian nickname only he used. "I remember the first time I laid eyes on you." He looked at Nick like he might cry, which made

Nick want to escape to somewhere, anywhere. His dad was too sentimental. Nick touched the gift in his front pocket and wondered what it was. "Can I ask you something?"

"Sure. Anything."

"Do you think about her sometimes?"

He was positive his father knew exactly what he was talking about. His mother always floated in this empty space between them. "Yes," his father said softly. "And you look more like her every birthday. Especially those eyes. Her entire clan had them."

His father walked over to him and looked like he might hug him, but he ended up just patting Nick on the shoulder.

Nick sighed. Failed magician or not—make that the world's worst magician with very bad jokes—he was still his dad. "I'll see you in the morning."

"Bright and early. We can go together to pick out a brand-new skateboard for your birthday, just like I promised. Something rad."

"Rad?"

"Just trying to get with the lingo. 'Night, Kolya."

Nick went into his room—only big enough for a twin bed and a small dresser with his TV and video-game console on top. He turned on the light and pulled the present out of his pocket. He unwrapped it; inside was a small, black leather box with a gold crest embossed on the top of it. All right, he had been hoping for a new game for his game system, but the crest was still cool. Holding his breath, he opened the box.

Nestled on a velvet cushion was a thick gold chain, and dangling from it hung a golden key about two inches long, the top part of which was a perfect circle. In the center of the circle were letterings in a strange script Nick couldn't read. The key shape itself—the part that would go into a lock— was elaborate, intricate. Nick wondered what it opened. A safety-deposit box? His dad was always broke—they didn't own anything you'd need a safety-deposit box for. Maybe the key opened nothing, but it was fun to imagine it opened a treasure. He wished he could read the lettering. Maybe that would tell him what it opened. He'd have to ask Grandpa.

Nick pulled the chain and key over his head, and it slid between his shirt and skin, falling to his chest where his heart beat. When the key touched his bare skin, it felt warm. Suddenly, a strange sort of buzzing pulsated in his chest, like a hive of bees.

His room began spinning around and around until he couldn't even focus on anything and he thought he'd throw up. He held on to his bed, trying to concentrate on the blue bedspread but seeing only a blur. And then, as suddenly as the world had started to move, it stopped. He heard something. A thumping sound.

"Dad?" he called out.

Instead, the handle to his closet door turned, and the magician Damian stepped through. Nick shook his head. Damian looked like he did in all his posters, tall, with long black hair and pale eyes. Nick blinked hard, but Damian was still there.

"I must be dreaming," he whispered, his heart pounding so hard, he wondered if that had been the thumping sound he heard.

"'Fraid not, Nicholai. Time to fly," Damian said, waving his hand, and that was the last thing Nick remembered.

THE FAMILY TREE

ICK WOKE UP ON A BROCADE-COVERED COUCH IN AN immense library, a luxuriously soft blanket covering him. He rubbed his eyes and tried to remember what had happened. Instinctively, he put his hand to his mother's necklace and the key—it was still there.

Nick remembered Grandpa taking him to the magic shop. His father's off-key singing. The leather box with the strange golden crest. The golden key. And then? Damian? None of it made sense.

He sat up. The room was cavernous, the ceiling so high he could barely make out the fanciful paintings that spanned across it like pictures of the Sistine Chapel ceiling he once saw in a book. Clouds and stars and fanciful palaces with flying people loomed over him, far away. He craned his neck.

He thought the clouds were moving. Blinking several times, he realized that they were! The clouds floated ever so slowly, as if a soft breeze was blowing them on a summer day. The stars twinkled. And occasionally, the flying people blinked. He had never seen anything like it.

The walls were lined with books. He stood and walked over to the shelves. Running his fingers along the spines, he noticed they were all thick, leather, and very old-looking. He blew at the spines and dust flew off, allowing him to read their print. Some were in foreign languages and different alphabets, or even just symbols. The ones he could read had names like *Book of Spells of the Ancient Egyptians*, *Magical Talismans of the Druids*, *Arbatel of Magick*, *Key of Solomon*, *Sword of Moses*, *Morgana's Spells of Fate*. He had no idea who the Druids or Morgana even were, but every book on every shelf, as far as he could see, was about magic.

He pulled one down and opened it, but it was written in a script he didn't understand.

"You'll learn to read that someday," a voice said.

Nick whirled around. "Damian!"

"In the flesh. No magical trick. Look." He stepped toward Nick and held out his hand. "Go ahead, pinch me."

Nick did. As hard as he could.

"Ouch! I said pinch me, not *maim* me."

"Take me home!" Nick shouted, backing up a step.

"Come on, you don't really want to go home. Not yet. Not until you find out what this," Damian waved his hand toward the room, "is all about. Not until you know why you could gaze into the crystal ball." He looked at Nick smugly.

Nick blinked. "You've kidnapped me! My dad has probably called the police. I bet my face is on TV right now. You won't get away with this."

Damian turned his back to him and walked over to a desk. "That doesn't concern me," he said arrogantly as he rifled through some papers.

Nick charged at him. "Doesn't concern you?" He swept a stack of papers onto the floor.

"Stop that! I heard you were a bit unruly…a *skateboarder*." He shuddered. "And those report cards. But no, it doesn't concern me. Your grandfather is, at this very moment, explaining the whole thing to your father so he doesn't fret. Now, we have a lot of work to do, so come along."

Nick's head swam. This was more confusing than math class, which he'd flunked. "My grandfather? He *knew* you were going to take me? That's really strange—even for him. I don't believe you."

Damian sighed, his green eyes flashing impatience. "But it's true, Kolya."

"How do you know me? And how do you know that's my father's nickname for me?"

29

"Because your mother was the one to give it to you."

"How do you know my mother? She's dead. She's been dead a really long time."

Damian walked over to his huge desk, which overflowed with papers, books, and, in one corner, a little white mouse in a golden cage.

"Here," he said, moving some papers out of the way and revealing a book so big Nick couldn't imagine how it ever could be moved. It was practically the size of the desk itself and looked as though it must weigh hundreds of pounds. Its leather was old and weathered, and Nick couldn't see a title written anywhere on it.

Damian opened it to the middle page, the paper thick and gilded on the edges but completely blank.

"This is the Tree."

Nick walked closer and peered at the page. He started to wonder if Damian was crazy like Madame B. or Grandpa. At first, nothing happened, but as Nick continued to watch, the pages stirred where they met in the binding. When the movement ceased there was a tiny plant, only an inch tall or so, sprouting directly from the page. Nick looked over to Damian with an expression begging for an explanation.

"I told you, skater boy. The Tree."

The tree grew—in miniature—its trunk twisting and turning, leaves sprouting, branches extending, vines curling around them. Roots grew and unfurled, swirling around the legs of the desk, until the tree stood about five feet tall rising from the middle of the book.

"You are...here." Damian pointed, and moved a few leaves. They rustled like real tree leaves.

Nick stared. He *was* there. A miniature head hung from the topmost branch like an apple. His own face. Its pale eyes blinked. Its mouth smiled.

"How did you do that? What is it? A hologram? Computer effects?"

Damian pursed his lips in a look of disgust. "Mirrors, computer effects. Those are for fakes and amateurs. They are for illusionists. Do you understand the difference between an illusionist and a magician?"

Nick shook his head, still mesmerized by the Tree.

"Illusion is smoke and mirrors. It's what those other magic acts do. It's how they fool the audience. How they deceive people into seeing things that aren't really there. This is different. What we do is something else entirely. It's magic."

"It looks so real...I can't believe it. And there's my mother!" Nick's throat tightened until it hurt. He swallowed hard and then whispered, "And my grandfather."

He leaned in so close that the leaves brushed his face. They smelled like a damp forest, like moss after a heavy rain. He stared at his mother's face. He had never seen his mother in anything but a flat photograph. "Can they talk?"

"Sometimes. If they're angry with me and have something to say, they let me know it, unfortunately."

"But I still don't understand."

Damian said, "They're our ancestors."

"Our?"

"You, as I said, are here." He pointed to the dangling Nick on the Tree. "We're third cousins."

"Cousins?"

Damian nodded and parted branches, revealing himself, hanging like a piece of fruit.

"Yes. Once removed, actually. Now come around here."

Nick walked with Damian to the other side of the desk. The tree was black on its other side. No fruit hung. No leaves. It was charred. Nick leaned in closer and smelled burned wood, acrid and pungent. "What happened here?"

"This is where our family tree split."

"Split?" He looked up at his newfound cousin, still marveling that he was related to Damian—*the* Damian. That a tree had grown from a book. And that the ceiling had clouds that moved.

"Yes. Magic, dear cousin, can be used for good. Or it can be used for evil. And here is where our lineage split. Rasputin… he is from this side."

"Who's he?"

"A history lesson is in order. I've heard about your social-studies grade."

Nick rolled his eyes. It was summer break. He was supposed to be free from history lessons. But Damian waved his hand and this time, in the midst of the charred tree, a man appeared.

"He's really creepy looking." Nick said, staring at the shadowy man, his eyes the same color as Nick's, his face swarthy and covered with a ragged beard.

"He wasn't always. But that look in his eyes? He became enamored of power. Consumed by it until he was insane. Worst of all, he told the mother of a very sick boy that he could cure him."

"Could he?"

"No. Magicians have many gifts, but that isn't one of them. But Rasputin told the Tsarina he could cure her son."

"Tsarina?" Madame B. had said that she read the crystal ball for the Tsarina.

"That is what the people of Russia called their king and queen, their emperor and empress, a long, long time ago—the Tsar and Tsarina. The last of the Tsars had a very sick son. And this man—Rasputin—he deceived the family. Eventually, he put his league in with this side of the tree, with darkness, and everything that dark magic entails. He left our family. He was banished."

Nick looked at the charred and ruined tree. "What does any of this have to do with me?"

"This side is looking for you. The Shadowkeepers."

Nick stared at the fire-ravaged branches and scarred trunk. Whoever did that to the Tree was not someone Nick wanted to meet. "Why?"

"Because you represent the strongest lineage on our side, the Magickeepers side. Your grandmother and great-grandmother on your mother's side were very powerful, with rare and special skills. Our side has been searching for you. And we found you. And if we can find you, they can, too."

"And what happens if they find me?"

"We won't speak of that." Damian knocked on his desk three times and then spat over his left shoulder three times.

"Gross. Why did you just spit?"

"Russian custom. When you speak of something evil, you spit. Now we speak of good. You are to come with me, to live among us. Your clan. Your people. From your mother's side. You will be a part of my show."

Nick had passed Damian's billboard and fantastical hotel and casino thousands of times, always wondering how he did some of his famous illusions. But this was all far stranger than anything he could have imagined.

"Your show? But..."

"It's done. You will apprentice with me this summer. We can protect you. It will give us a chance to lure the Shadowkeepers into the light of day, where we can defeat them. Las Vegas is a city of nighttime. The Shadowkeepers thrive here. But we will root them out. Only then will you be safe."

Nick again looked at the Tree's destruction. This time he shuddered.

"Oh, and I almost forgot," Damian said.

"What?"

He handed Nick a crystal ball the size of a baseball. "Happy birthday, little cousin."

Just like at Madame B.'s, Nick couldn't see anything at first. He took a deep breath and tried to see with his mind like the old woman had taught him. When he gazed again, he saw his mother and father singing "Happy Birthday" to him. One candle was on the cake—a baby sat in a high chair. *Nick* was that baby. It was like watching a home movie.

Nick swallowed hard. "Thank you," he whispered. He turned, but Damian was gone. Turning to look at the desk, the Tree had disappeared and the book now sat closed, no indication remaining of the wonder it contained except for the faint smell of charred wood.

Nick shook his head. "This," he said to the little mouse on the desk, who stared at him with beady pink eyes, "has been the strangest birthday ever."

THIS CAN'T BE BREAKFAST?!

ICK SPENT THE NIGHT ON THE COUCH IN THE LIBRARY, staring up at the ceiling, which twinkled like the real Milky Way. He found the stars strangely comforting, yet also loneliness-inducing. Though he was tired, it was impossible to settle down. His mind raced with a million questions. Nothing that happened on his thirteenth birthday made any sense at all. Sometime in the night, though, exhaustion overtook him, and he dozed fitfully.

When Nick awoke, Damian stared down at him, glancing periodically at his gold pocket watch and impatiently tapping his foot.

"No sleeping in."

"But it's summer."

"Meaningless. Let's go."

Nick rubbed the sleep out of his eyes, sat up, and stretched. "What is that *stench?*" Nick wrinkled up his nose.

Damian ignored the question. "Come along, cousin." He turned, walked across the room, and opened the door. Nick threw aside the blanket and ran after him. When Nick poked his head through the doorway, he discovered he was actually in one of the most mysterious and most written about places in the world: on one of the top three floors of the Winter Palace Hotel and Casino, where, according to newspapers and magazines, Damian and members of his show lived full-time.

Nick trailed after Damian. "What is that? It's disgusting! Don't you smell it?"

"We prefer food from our homeland. That *stench* you're referring to is going to be *your* breakfast. Crepes."

"I love crepes." In fact, he had eaten crepes at many all-you-can-eat brunches with Grandpa. "But that sure doesn't smell like any I've eaten before."

"These are stuffed with sour cream and caviar."

"Caviar? As in those little fish eggs?" Nick's stomach flip-flopped.

"Of course! From the finest sturgeon. Come along. You've eaten your last cheeseburger. Time to eat the food you were *destined* to eat."

"For breakfast?" All he wanted was a bowl of cold cereal

and milk. Pancakes smothered in syrup. He'd even take one of his dad's soggy waffles. But fish eggs?

Nick walked down the very long hallway with carpeting so thick that his sneakers sank down into it. To his right was a bank of windows, and it was snowing outside. That was one of the mysteries of Las Vegas. Clouds hung around the Winter Palace, and from the clouds, a steady snow fell as thick as a blizzard—even on the hottest days of summer. It melted before it touched the sidewalk below, but nonetheless, when hotel guests looked out their windows, they saw pristine snow drifting from the sky. The hotel carefully guarded the manner in which the snow was made. Now was Nick's chance to find out.

"So how do you make the snow fall? Is there a snow machine somewhere? On the roof?" Nick knew investigative journalists had been hunting for the source of the snow for years.

Damian stopped in his tracks and turned around to glare at his little cousin. "*It's magic*. It's not some Disneyland trick. Everything you see here on these top floors is magic. And all of it is real. *Do not doubt what you see,* Nicholai. This is where you belong. It's where you've always belonged. These are no illusions." He swept his hand toward the windows. "Magic." Then he started down the hall again, his long stride meaning Nick had to struggle to keep up.

"Magic," Nick whispered to himself. "But they've never heard of air freshener?" The closer they got to the end of the hall, the more horrific it smelled.

Damian opened a door. "This is your bedroom. I had them prepare it for you."

Nick peered in. "Wow…" All his life, he had lived with his father in whatever hotel his dad worked at. His room in the Pendragon was so small that he had just a narrow foot of space between the bed and the dresser (just enough to slide out a shirt from the bottom drawer). Not the case here—this room was *huge*. The ornate furniture was intricately carved. The four-poster bed had tigers and bears carved into forest scenes, and the mattress was covered with a dark purple, velvet bedspread with gold threads running through it. Nick walked in and stood next to the bed.

"What's the crest?" he asked, pointing to the bedspread. The same crest was on the box his grandfather had given him.

"Our family's crest." Damian stood next to him.

Nick thought of showing Damian the necklace that had been his mother's but decided against it. Instead, he looked around the room. "Everything in here looks really, really old. And breakable," he said, spying a set of bookshelves, some of them holding gold-and-jeweled eggs and porcelain boxes.

"These are your heirlooms. Everything in here was once in your mother's room when she was a girl. And before her, your grandmother's. And before her, your great-grandmother's."

Nick blinked hard several times. All he and his father had of his mother were old costumes and some photographs. He moved toward the dresser and touched its gleaming surface, the burled wood polished so shiny he could almost see his reflection in it. He walked over to the closet and opened it. "What are these?"

"Your clothes."

"*These* aren't my clothes. Where are my T-shirts? My jeans? You've got to be kidding me if you think I'm wearing this stuff." Crisply starched white shirts hung next to shiny black dress pants that he wouldn't be caught *dead* wearing.

"But you will. Now come along to breakfast. You can change before school."

"Whoa. Wait one minute. It's *summer break*."

Damian faced him, eyes flecked with anger. "Listen to me, little cousin, there is no summer break for the Shadowkeepers. They're looking for you. They're looking to destroy the rest of the clan once and for all. There is no break. Ever again. *This* is your life now."

"I didn't ask for this to be my life. My life was just fine."

"It may have been fine, but it wasn't your destiny."

"Destiny? Who writes your dialogue, dude? Destiny? My destiny was to ride my skateboard and spend the summer goofing off. What's the point of coming to live at the Winter Palace Casino, being part of your show, living in a room like this, if I have to go to school? If I have to wear weird clothes and eat crepes with fish eggs?" Nick looked around. "If I have no television. No video games. No…cheeseburgers. My skateboard is back home. I don't even know if my dad will remember to feed my goldfish. He's probably floating belly up."

He expected Damian to yell at him—and he didn't care. Summer school? He'd rather spend the summer locked in his old room than go to school, so Damian could yell all he wanted.

Instead, Damian walked over to him and patted his shoulder. "Look, you have a lot to learn. The ways of the clan, our history, magic."

"I get to learn magic?" Now *that* could be interesting. "Real magic?" He thought of the snow falling. If he could learn how to do stuff like that, it would almost be worth fish eggs for breakfast.

Damian nodded. "You begin after breakfast. You'll see. Now come meet the family."

Nick followed as they went back out into the hall. The stench was even more overpowering there. Nick detected the pungent odor of cabbage. Lots and lots of cabbage.

Damian opened a door, and Nick screamed and took two steps backward. An enormous white tiger pounced at him, its face coming so close to his that he felt its damp whiskers and smelled its faintly fishy breath.

"Sascha!" A thin girl who looked a little younger than Nick, with long brown hair and pale blue eyes, snapped her fingers. "Come!"

Nick's heart pounded so hard, he could barely hear her. All he could concentrate on was the hot breath of the tiger. The animal turned its head to gaze at the girl, faced Nick again with what he swore was a promise that he would be eaten later, and retreated to the girl's side.

With a little distance between him and the tiger, Nick sized it up. Even sitting on its haunches, the tiger was taller than the girl standing next to it.

"What the…?" he said, breathless.

"Sorry," the girl said, wrapping an arm around the tiger's thick neck and rubbing her face against its fur. "Sascha is a tad mistrustful of strangers."

"Nicholai, meet your cousin, Isabella. Second cousin, actually."

The girl stuck her hand out. "Nice to meet you."

Nick didn't move. "If I shake your hand, is that tiger going to bite mine off?"

The girl laughed. "Don't be ridiculous. Sascha obeys me. You are perfectly safe. Come meet her properly."

Tentatively, Nick stepped across the hall and shook Isabella's hand.

"Go ahead. Pet her. She's really a giant pussycat. *If* I want her to be."

Nick petted the giant tiger on the head. Her fur was the softest, most velvety thing he had ever touched. His fingers slid down into the fur, disappearing in its richness. His heart pounded at being so close to such a powerful animal. The tiger stood perfectly still. "How is she so well-trained?"

Isabella looked at him with disdain. "What a silly question."

Nick rolled his eyes. He hated when anyone talked down to him. "Right. Magic."

"Come along," Damian said. "Breakfast. Then you two have school."

Nick glanced over at the girl with the tiger. Great. Now he had to go to school with her. And probably the tiger, who, though totally cool, was still staring at him like he was breakfast.

Sighing, Nick followed Damian into the dining room. Inside was a long table that probably could seat a hundred people under a chandelier that dripped with crystals. The table was laden with a feast on silver platters, steaming plates of crepes and bowls full of caviar. Pastries and plates of fruit crowded the center of the table—though most of it looked like prunes and things he wouldn't eat if Damian paid him to do so. Ornate teapots stood on a sideboard.

Around the table sat people in costumes. The men wore pressed black pants and white shirts—like those that hung in Nick's closet. Some wore ornately embroidered, colorful vests. The women were costumed in elaborate dresses, and many wore heavy jewel necklaces. The dresses were all made of rich fabrics and lace inlaid with gemstones, the threads gleaming as if they were real gold. At the head of the table sat a woman who looked ancient—and yet not. She appeared to have fallen asleep, her head leaning back against her chair. Her hair was pure white and pulled into a bun like Nick had seen women wear in history books, with diamond-encrusted combs holding it into place. He could tell she was very old by her gnarled hands, which curled around a porcelain teacup painted with gold, and yet her face was unlined, with slightly pink powdered cheeks. Nick looked at them all, feeling as though he had stepped onto a movie set. As if he had stepped back in time.

"Everyone, this is Nicholai," Damian announced.

An assortment of greetings rang out from the people around the table. Then the eyes of the ancient woman opened wide. Her eyes were the same color as Nick's own.

"Grand Duchess," Damian bowed slightly. "This is Kolya." He lightly shoved Nick toward the head of the table. On either side of the woman sat two more tigers even bigger than Isabella's, yet they looked—well, old. Like the Grand Duchess herself. Their eyes also seemed wise. Ancient.

"He-ll-o," Nick stammered.

She crooked her finger at him. Nick walked closer.

"You have returned to us, Kolya," she whispered, her voice tremulous.

Nick nodded hesitantly and looked around the table. Everyone had stopped eating and drinking and was looking at him. Some smiled. A few women dabbed at their eyes with lace handkerchiefs.

"Eat!" the old woman snapped. She looked at the tigers on either side of her. "Make way," she commanded. Each tiger withdrew. One went to a corner and sat, like a sentinel. The other tiger moved under the table and curled at the old woman's feet. "Sit down," she told Nick. "By my side." She patted a chair.

Nick reached the stiff high-backed chair and sat down, the smell of fish, cabbage, and stewed prunes overwhelming him. He took small spoonfuls of food, his stomach rumbling with both hunger and disapproval of the menu.

He looked around for juice, but didn't see any. As if she had read his mind, the Grand Duchess snapped her fingers, and an ornate silver teapot rose from the sideboard and glided through the air, poising over a teacup in front of his plate. Nick looked down the table and saw that every dish sat in silver tureens and platters with silver legs and claw-shaped feet. No one passed plates. The plates and platters walked on their own to serve diners. Blinking back astonishment, he watched as the silver teapot tilted in mid-air. The darkest black liquid he had ever seen poured into his cup, steam rising.

"We drink tea, Kolya."

He lifted his teacup and took a sip. He almost spit it out. Not only did it burn his tongue, it was also bitter.

Nick set his teacup down and began eating, nearly gagging on his food. What he would have given for one of Grandpa's all-you-can-eat adventures!

Isabella and her tiger sat at the other end of the table. Periodically, she tossed bits of food in the air, which the tiger caught in her mouth. He wished he had a tiger that obeyed him like that. No one would tease him as the new kid in school if he had a tiger.

The Grand Duchess leaned back against her chair and appeared to fall asleep. Soon, Nick heard her soft snores. He continued eating, aware that family members were stealing surreptitious glances at him. He bowed his head and tried to avoid looking at any of them.

A short time later, a man entered the room dressed in long black robes. He wore dark, horn-rimmed glasses, and his black hair was cropped close to his head.

"Isabella...Nicholai," he announced. "Time for school." He clapped his hands like he was a king. "Come!"

Inwardly, Nick groaned. If he were at home, he would

still be in bed watching cartoons and eating sugary cereal right from the box. This was shaping up to be the worst summer ever.

REVELATIONS AND
ADVERTISEMENTS

*T*HIS IS OUR CLASSROOM?" NICK SURVEYED THE ROOM WHERE he and Isabella were to be tutored privately. It reminded him of Madame B.'s, full of books and jars of strange ingredients. Just as in the library, some of the books were not only in different languages, but different alphabets. The jars were filled with powders in every shade of the rainbow, and liquids—some of which glowed ominously. Spiders—big, fat, hairy spiders that gave him the creeps—sat in jars, their legs twitching, webs spinning up to the lids that Nick hoped were on tight. Mice in gilded cages sat on their haunches, staring at him and occasionally running their tiny paws over their whiskers. As Nick walked, they turned their heads as if they were watching him.

His teacher sat at a large wooden desk at the front of the room, its legs ornately carved like tree trunks twisted with vine. The teacher's robes billowed up around him as he settled into his high-backed chair, as huge as a throne, and he pointed to two smaller desks in front of him.

"I am Theo, Damian's brother. Today, Kolya, you begin your journey into magic."

Nick narrowed his eyes, looking closely at Theo. "That makes us cousins, too, then?"

Theo nodded. "You are related to everyone in the clan either by blood or marriage. Now, we must begin. You have a lot of catching up to do."

Isabella leaned her elbows on her desk. Her tiger sprawled on the floor, looking like a large rug. She breathed slowly and steadily, occasionally twitching her nose and once even curling her mouth into a smile, as if having a dream.

"And I'm really going to learn magic?"

Theo nodded. "But as with all lessons, we must learn from the past. We must look backward before we can cast our eyes forward. Isn't that right, Isabella?"

She sighed. "Yes, Theo." She turned to look at Nick. "You'll learn very quickly that Theo loves history. It's his favorite subject."

Theo waved his hand and said something in what Nick guessed was Russian, and a crystal ball—bigger even than Madame B.'s—floated through the air, then settled on a pedestal on the corner of Theo's desk.

Theo looked at Nick and Isabella and winked. "Ordinary teachers have projectors and chalkboards. I have this. Behold…the *watchmaker*."

Nick stared as the ball grew smoky, then turned a rich amethyst color, then red, and finally, as if a curtain had parted, the ball was clear. Inside it, two men dressed in what were clearly old-fashioned clothes began speaking. Nick leaned closer. Tools, gears, and hundreds of clocks in various states of repair (or disrepair) littered the walls and long wooden tables. Clearly, this was a watchmaker's shop.

✧　✧　✧

Tours, France, 1824
"But tell me, Monsieur Houdin," the man said, his accent thick with a Russian edge. "How does it work?"

The watchmaker, Jean Houdin, smiled enigmatically, his hair slightly askew and wild looking. "Magic."

"But tell me." The man's eyes were a pale, almost translucent blue, and he wore an elegant black suit. The buttons and cuff links were glittering rubies.

"The watch stops time itself. Its spell, my magical friend, will give you approximately thirty seconds. Thirty precious seconds of time, while everyone around you is frozen, with no memory of time stopping. None. Think of the illusions you could do. Think of them. You will be the toast of Paris. Your entire clan will be hailed throughout Europe."

The man shook his head. "We do not seek notoriety. We do not seek fame. We seek only to develop our art."

"But I have heard," Houdin whispered, "that you are favored by Tsar Alexander. That you travel with the royal family. That your own quarters in the palace are beyond the imaginings of a simple watchmaker like me. Velvet and satin, jewels and gold-encrusted plates. I have heard that Tsar Alexander relies on you, on your crystal balls."

The man with the ruby cuff links grew somber, almost menacing. "Do not believe all that you hear, watchmaker."

"Just once, I would like to gaze into a ball. To see what... you can see."

"Only those of the bloodline can." The man took the watch—a pocket watch made of pure gold—from Houdin and turned it over and over in his palm. "I will make you a deal, Houdin."

"Yes?"

"I will trade you. My hourglass...for your watch." The man in the cape lifted a handsome leather trunk onto the table where the watchmaker was displaying the watch. The Russian unlocked the trunk and withdrew a large hourglass with writing around its rim. "I wish to join modern times.

It's 1824! I wish to have a watch, not an *hourglass.* That is what I want."

Houdin leaned close to the hourglass. "The sand...it looks like it is gold."

"Indeed it is. This hourglass is priceless."

Inside the hourglass, the golden sand swirled, like a Saharan sandstorm, spinning and moving, endlessly shifting shape.

"It is magnificent!" Houdin touched the engraved rim. "Look how the sand moves as if wind stirs within the glass! The magic of it. The craftsmanship..."

The Russian smiled. "Do we have a deal?"

Houdin was mesmerized by the swirling sand. "I don't know."

The Russian withdrew a small velvet sack from his pants pocket. "Look within."

Houdin opened the bag and peered inside. He gasped aloud. "That diamond is the size of a quail's egg."

"Do we have a deal then?"

Houdin nodded.

"Tell me how to cast its spell."

Houdin leaned in close and whispered in the man's ear.

The Russian smiled. He opened the watch. He pulled on its fob, stopping the motion of the second hand. Then he said, "*Je suis le roi de temps.*"

Houdin instantly froze. He appeared to not move or blink—or even breathe. The Russian smiled and collected his diamond. He left the hourglass on the table and laughed out loud at his own trickery. He exited the shop, whistling to himself, and entered the busy street as a horse-drawn carriage rushed past him.

A few moments later, Houdin moved again. He shook his head and yawned. Then he looked at the hourglass. He furrowed his brow.

"Now how did this get here?" he asked himself. Then he squinted, a look of wonderment on his face.

"The diamond!" he shouted aloud to only his many watches and clocks. "My pocket watch!"

He ran out to the street, craning his head in either direction. Horses drawing carriages clip-clopped by on the cobblestone streets. But the man in the cloak was gone.

And the hourglass stood, its gold sand glittering in the lamplight on the watchmaker's table.

✧ ✧ ✧

"That man," Theo pointed, as the figures in the crystal ball started to fade, "the man in the cloak, he was my great-great-grandfather."

"Do you mean to tell me," Nick said, "that going way back in time, our relatives were liars and cheats?" Nick thought the pocket watch that the man stole looked remarkably like the one Damian owned. Thieves! His family was from a long line of thieves.

"Let me ask you something, Nicholai," Theo said, clasping his hands together. "When you go to a museum, where do you think those artifacts came from?"

Nick shrugged. "I never thought about it. And I think I've only been to a museum once anyway. And it was boring."

"Boring? Clearly, you don't know the first thing about museums. That will change now that I'm in charge of your education instead of your father." He sighed. "*Americans!* Well, antiquities, my dear Kolya, have been robbed and stolen, gained by trickery and forgery, and even murder, throughout time. Magic relics are no different."

"Magic relics?"

He nodded. "Magic takes many forms. The relics can make some spells more powerful, more potent. My great-great-grandfather foolishly believed he was becoming part of modern society by trading the hourglass for the watch. But in reality, the Eternal Hourglass was far more powerful than he even realized. He never should have let Houdin get his hands on it."

"Who was Houdin?"

"An illusionist. The father of modern illusions. Trickery with ether, sleight of hand, and magnets and automatons."

"Was he related to Harry Houdini?"

"Houdini took his stage name from Houdin."

"So was the watchmaker a Magickeeper?"

"He wasn't one of us, but he bribed and traded for magic relics. After the hourglass was traded, it then switched hands many times throughout history—and has been lost to us. Like so many of our relics. We spend a great deal of time hunting for them. The lesson here, Kolya, is that we learn from the past. We must honor and treasure every bit of our magic as sacred."

"THEO!" The crystal ball filled with a lavender smoky mist, and a man's face appeared inside it, swarthy, with huge dark eyebrows that perched like furry caterpillars over pale blue eyes.

Theo rolled his eyes. "Not now, Sergei."

"PLEASE!" The face in the crystal ball looked directly at Nick. "Nicholai, tell your cousin that I am the best horse trader in Russia!"

Nick leaned closer to the crystal ball and touched it, not knowing what to expect. The head inside looked so real. "Excuse me?" He looked over at Isabella, then Theo, then back at the head inside the ball. "You said my name. Am I supposed to know you?"

"Yes. I am trying to sell him a horse for you. A special horse. For the show. An *Akhal-Teke!* For real!" The man's face disappeared, and suddenly, Nick was gazing at a field filled with horses. Then the man's head popped into the crystal ball.

"Shop at CRAZY SERGEI'S horse lot. Where my prices are INSANE!" He gestured with his hands and crossed his eyeballs. "INSANE!"

"Get out of my ball, Sergei!" Theo ordered. "Or I will never buy a horse from you again." He crossed his arms, a stern expression on his face.

"Fine!" Sergei said. "But this Akhal-Teke...I will sell it to the next person who comes to me with an offer. You know they are a dying breed. Maybe three thousand left in the entire world. And I have a golden one waiting for the new apprentice himself."

"Enough, Sergei. Or I'll tell Damian. And then no one in the entire clan will buy horses from you. Ever."

"Fine! I go now. But Nicholai. Think about it." At that, the ball went dark.

"What was that?" Nick asked.

"Commercial," Isabella yawned.

"Commercial?"

"In a manner of speaking, yes," Theo replied.

"I don't need a horse."

"Yes, you do," Isabella said.

"For what?"

"For the show," she said, bored, as if it was the most obvious answer in the world.

"Wh-what do you mean, for the show?" Nick stammered.

"Damian thought of it," Isabella said.

Theo nodded. "You look like him."

"Yeah, so?"

"So," Theo said, "in my brother's sheer audacity and genius, he's decided the best way to incorporate you into the show as his apprentice is for you to play a younger version of him on stage."

"I don't get it."

"Look," Isabella said. "You're going to play Damian. You'll ride on stage on a horse, do some spectacular magic. The audience will love it."

"Audience? Look, I don't even like it when I'm called on in class and have to read something out loud. I thought I was going to be backstage."

Theo shook his head. "Impossible. It is your destiny to be on stage."

Nick exhaled loudly. "Look, yesterday, I was a kid with a skateboard, a cheeseburger, and a sense of purpose about summer."

"Purpose?" Theo laughed. "What purpose was that?"

"What every kid in the whole world's purpose is during the summer. Sleep in. Goof off. Don't you people understand?

It's like…it's like practically the law. And I come here and you keep talking about destiny and now relics and a magic hourglass, and none of it makes any sense."

"You can't fight destiny," Theo said softly. "Destiny is a part of who you are, my young cousin."

"But I don't want to be in the show."

Isabella stared at him. "You don't understand. This is what we do. You have to be part of it."

Nick shook his head. "I can't do magic like Damian."

"But you're going to learn," Theo said calmly.

"And I can't ride a horse."

"You'll learn that, too," Theo replied.

"And not just any horse." Isabella grinned. "An Akhal-Teke."

"What's that?"

"They gleam. Their coats look metallic, like real gold. And they can ride across the desert without water. Like a camel," Isabella said. "Perfect for Las Vegas!"

"You have the wrong kid. I've never ridden a horse in my life."

"You will learn, cousin. You will learn," Theo smiled, nodding. "You and your horse will be a magnificent addition to the show."

There was a soft knock on the door, followed by a tall woman entering the classroom.

"You must be Nicholai," she said. Her long black hair was woven into a thick braid that fell to the small of her back. Her eyes were pale—but instead of blue, like Nick's, they were flecked with green and gold, which matched her deep green, flowing dress, the collar embroidered with threads that glinted in the light.

He nodded, and she approached him, leaned down, and kissed him once on each cheek, the way he once saw French tourists greet each other in the hotel.

"I am Irina," she said, her accent thick—like Madame B.'s.

"Am I related to you, too?"

"Of course, *dorogoi*. Your mother was my best friend—and my cousin."

Nick wondered why he had never met a single person from his extended family before.

"When you were in a cradle, I came to visit you. While your Papa was out. Such a precious little baby. Your mother…so happy." Irina's eyes grew wet. "I cannot speak of such things now." She walked over to Theo's wooden desk, knocked three times, and spat over her left shoulder three times. Nick tried not to stare, but really, he still didn't understand why they spit over bad news.

"Now we speak of good. I am grateful you have come home to us." She turned to Isabella. "Come along, Sister. You and Sascha have rehearsal."

Isabella stood. Sascha lifted her immense head, licked one paw, stretched, and then rose. The tiger, her white fur and black stripes luscious and full, immediately fell in step beside Isabella, claws making a scraping noise as they scratched the polished wood floors, muscles rippling.

Nick faced Theo. "Can I get a tiger?"

Theo shook his head. "Only the women in the lineage have power over animals."

Nick bit his lip. "What about a lion?"

Theo shook his head again. "Only Isabella can have a cat."

"Sascha is a lot bigger than a cat!"

"Still, only the women. Irina is in charge of the animals."

"But you just said I have to learn to ride a horse. That's an animal."

"You have to learn to ride your horse—just like an ordinary human."

"I was afraid of that."

"But no horse today. No, instead today, you and I must attend to your first magic lesson. Today, you are going to move this." From beneath his desk, he pulled out a small gilded cage. Inside, a hedgehog nestled on a soft nest of grass. Next, Theo pulled out a second cage. An empty cage.

"Move it? What do you mean move it?"

"You are going to move the hedgehog from this cage to this one." Theo pointed. "Using magic."

"You have *got* to be kidding me. What? Do I say a few magic words?"

"Each magician must use his own magic words."

"Okay. So what are mine?"

"I can't tell you what yours are."

"Why not?"

"Each magician must find his words on his own. Must give his own voice to the magic within."

"Well, do I get a magic wand?"

"No wand. We don't need one. Not that they work anyway. Occasionally, but they are unreliable. Please? You think we are like…a sideshow? We are real magicians. Wands are for amateurs."

"All right, then." Nick looked at the hedgehog. It made a sniffling noise and stared up at him with beady little black eyes. "Abracadabra!"

Nothing happened. Except Theo laughed. Loudly. He laughed so hard, his eyes were wet with tears.

"It's the only magic word I know!"

"Come on. How about hocus pocus?" Theo said, then slapped his hand on the table and howled with laughter all over again.

"I've never done this before!"

"First of all, cousin, you might try *krax pex phax*."

"What kind of magic word is that?"

"It's from our family. Our spell. It means, *I create as I speak*. It has some power."

"Fine. *Krax pex phax*," Nick said, repeating the words exactly as Theo said them, which sounded like *kreks peks feks*.

Still nothing.

"This isn't working."

"No kidding," Theo said.

Nick glared at Theo. "I don't know how to move your stupid hedgehog! This is the dumbest thing ever! This is magic?" He leaned down close to the hedgehog and said, "Just move! Disappear!"

And then it did.

Nick jumped backward, knocking over a chair and nearly falling on the ground, his heart pounding. He had blinked, and it was gone. He looked all around. He even looked under the desk, but he didn't see the hedgehog anywhere. It was no longer in its cage.

"Where'd it go?"

"Someplace." Theo smiled. "Now you just need to bring it back and put it in this cage over here."

"Bring it back? I don't even know how I got it to move in the first place."

"Yes, you do. Think, Kolya."

Nick shook his head. "Honestly. I don't know how I did it. Did *you* do it?" Maybe it was all a trick to make him think he had magical powers—the crystal ball at Madame B.'s, the hedgehog; maybe all of it was fake.

"Of course I didn't do it." Theo stared meaningfully at him. "It starts here." Theo pointed at his stomach. "When you laugh, you feel this joy inside. Right there. You feel it bubble up inside. Think of something happy. It starts there. When you are nervous, you get butterflies. You feel it flutter inside. If you are very nervous, it's more like bat wings beating against your rib cage. When you are angry, it starts there, too. Like a ball of heat and fire. With magicians, our power starts in the same place."

"I don't get it."

"You will. You'll learn to train that feeling, to use it, to direct it. And then, you will arrive at your greatness."

"I don't want to arrive at greatness."

"It doesn't matter. Sometimes greatness finds you. Now," Theo handed Nick the empty cage where he was supposed to magically rematerialize the hedgehog. "I suggest you lock yourself in your room and work on bringing back your pet hedgehog. He is probably somewhere cold and lonely. Hedgehogs don't like the cold at all."

"My pet hedgehog?"

"Yes. His name is Vladimir."

"So how come Isabella gets a tiger? And I get a hedgehog? If I'm destined for greatness, why do I get a small, rat-looking thing with beady eyes and needles sticking out of his back and *she* gets a white tiger that follows her around?"

"Questions for another day. Be off with you."

Handing Nick the cage, Theo stood, nodded, and disappeared. Disappeared just like that, with only the faint rustling sound of his robes remaining.

"They have got to be kidding me!" Nick shouted. He looked around the classroom, then took the cage, and stomped off down the hall to his own room.

They could abracadabra and hocus pocus him all they wanted, but he wasn't destined for greatness. He was destined to get out of this crazy hotel and away from disappearing hedgehogs and horse dealers in crystal balls.

JUST A DIP
IN THE POOL

*B*Y MIDNIGHT. NICK'S HEDGEHOG STILL HAD NOT reappeared in its cage. Nick had skipped dinner, which he now realized was a mistake, even if dinner did smell like cabbage and old socks. His stomach rumbled with hunger and displeasure. If Theo was right and magic started somewhere down in his gut, then he was in trouble, because all he could think about was how much he wanted a cheeseburger.

He sat cross-legged on his bed and stared at the empty cage.

"Come on, you stupid hedgehog! Come back!"

But the cage stood empty.

Then he heard a faint knock on his door. "If it's you, Damian," he called out, "just zap through the door or whatever the heck it is you do."

"Nick, it's me, Isabella," a whispered voice replied.

Nick climbed off his bed, walked to the door, and opened it. Isabella stood there, in a wet suit, with Sascha next to her. His cousin had on flippers. And a snorkel mask. A beach towel was wrapped around Sascha's neck.

"What the...?"

Isabella pushed the snorkel mask up onto her forehead. "Come swim with us. But you can't tell anyone."

"Swim? Where?"

"In the swimming pool."

"Okay. But won't the hotel guests freak out just a little when they see a tiger swimming? And isn't the dive suit overkill?"

"Not for our pool," she grinned. "The family pool is a little different from the pool the guests use." She held out a black rubber wet suit. "This one belonged to Peter, one of our cousins. He grew almost a foot this year, and it doesn't fit him anymore. Come on. Put it on. I'll wait."

Nick nodded and shut the door, stripped out of his jeans and T-shirt—the last remnants of his old life—and pulled on the wet suit, which stuck to his skin as he wriggled into it. Finally, the rubber wet suit was on, fitting like a glove.

He grabbed his room key from the dresser and opened the door. Sascha eyed him and offered a low growl.

"Shh!" Isabella put her fingers to her lips. The tiger immediately quieted. Isabella looked at Nick. "What do you need your key for?"

"To open my door."

"Silly. No you don't. Go ahead and shut it."

Nick pulled the door closed.

"*Osnovyvat,*" she commanded. The door swung wide.

"Whoa! What did you say?"

"I told your door to open."

"Teach me how."

"You just speak it—but you must say it like you already believe it has happened. You picture in your head whatever it is you want to happen—as if it were already true. Concentrate. Magic knows if you don't believe."

Nick shut the door. Then he repeated the Russian word she'd taught him. "*Osnovyvat.*" The door swung open. "This is totally awesome."

Isabella nodded. "I haven't had to make my bed in years."

"You have a spell to make your bed?"

She nodded. "I'll teach it to you. I do it every morning. Except on exam days, of course."

"What do you mean?"

"On days when Theo gives an exam, I don't make my bed. It's bad luck."

"Is that kind of like the spitting three times thing?"

She nodded. "It's best not to tempt fate, you know? Now, come on. Time for our swim. Quietly."

She tiptoed down the thick-carpeted hallway dimly lit by sconces on the walls. Through the windows, the bright lights of Las Vegas blinked and danced. Nick watched the snow falling on the casino, never tiring of its beauty as fat, pristine flakes occasionally landed against the glass, frozen for a second before melting. He followed Isabella as she turned a corner, then another corner. Finally, they came to a door with a brass plaque on it that read, "POOL."

She opened the door with her command, and Nick followed her into darkness. She quickly shut the door again and fastened a deadbolt. He couldn't see anything. The pool room was dark, but he heard splashing and water lapping. And he heard breathing.

"Why is it so cold in here?" He shivered. "Aren't most hotel pools so hot it feels like a bathtub?"

"Not this one," she laughed and flicked on the lights that illuminated the pool. Suddenly, the water glowed with a greenish light, and Nick gasped.

"Polar bears!"

Isabella nodded. "They're going to be part of the new show. The story line will have Damian escaping from Siberia, crossing the Bering Strait, and fighting off polar bears. And here they are."

Nick had never even seen a live polar bear before, let alone polar bears swimming a few feet away from him. Three of them swam. As each of them dove through the water, they looked at least ten feet tall. Their paws were bigger than his head. And they had big...sharp...claws.

"Please tell me they're like Sascha. That they're tame. I don't want to be polar bear food."

Isabella nodded. "Irina and I have been working with them. Come on, let's go swimming. Sascha, stay."

The tiger flopped down to the tiled floor and rested her head on her paws. Isabella took a running leap toward the pool and did a cannonball into the water.

Nick held his breath, half-expecting her to be eaten alive. She was underwater for a while, then suddenly shot to the surface screaming. He started toward the pool but then realized her scream was actually a squeal of laughter. A polar bear came up from beneath her and hoisted her on its shoulders. She rested her head against its neck.

"Come on in. The wet suit will keep you warm."

Nick peered into the pool. It was Olympic-sized—at least— with deep blue tiles embossed with the family crest in gold. Blocks of ice floated and bobbed and created a kind of steam as they melted. A polar bear swam by him and then turned on its back. Nick got a good look at its teeth. They were huge. But he sure wasn't going to let a *girl* know he was chicken.

Shutting his eyes, he let out a yelp and did a cannonball into the icy water.

Even with the wet suit, when his face hit the water, it knocked the air out of his lungs. He kicked his legs and thrust toward the surface, gulping in air when he emerged.

"Holy cow! That's freezing!"

Isabella reclined on the belly of a polar bear, using it like a raft as it paddled on its back across the water.

"Well, there is *ice* floating in here, Nick. What did you expect? That's why you have the wet suit."

Know-it-all.

"Mischa!" Isabella sat up. A polar bear with enormous black eyes approached her. "Let Nicholai ride on you. It will keep him warm."

Before he had a chance to protest, the bear had lifted him like a rag doll out of the water and flipped him. Then the bear floated on his back, with Nick resting on his enormous belly.

She was right. He slid his hand through the bear's fur. It was so thick he couldn't see his own fingers, and water repelled off it, gathering in thick droplets. The bear was warm and radiated heat. They splashed and floated, and Nick forgot he was cold.

"Now this is cool. A lot cooler than class with Theo."

"Theo isn't so bad, Nick. Despite all the history he'll make us sit through. He is a brilliant magician, too." She dropped her voice to a whisper. "Even better, I think, than Damian."

"Well, then why does he just teach? Why isn't he in the show? Why isn't he the star of the show?"

"I'm not sure." She slipped onto her stomach so she was nose to nose with her bear. "He once said that it was more important that the history of magic live on, that the secrets and craft go on, than the show. The show is just how we blend in."

"But why blend in? I mean, if we're so powerful, if you can just command a door to open, or Damian can push a sword through a woman on stage and turn her into a dove, or I can make something disappear, why should we hide that?"

"More history. Ever learn about the Salem witch trials when you were in school?"

"Wasn't that when the Puritans thought people were witches? And put them on trial and then killed them? They were scared of them."

"Yes. But the women on trial were Magickeepers who had come to America. They called them witches, but they were like us."

"That's not in the history books."

"Of course not. Only the Magickeepers know—the historians like Theo who want to preserve the past. Mary I of England—she also executed many magicians. For heresy."

"But our family is from Russia, not England."

She nodded. "Yes, but we're all from ancient Egypt, a bloodline of Magickeepers. Eventually, we scattered all over the globe. Our clan went to Russia and stayed. Others are in England. France. Japan. Nearly every country. But we all went underground when the persecutions became bad."

"But we're not exactly hidden. We've got snow falling on the casino."

"When the family bought the casino, they thought hiding ourselves as a magic act was brilliant. We're here, but we're hidden in a way. And that's how we protect ourselves from the Shadowkeepers. We're safe here. Right in the spotlight. No one suspects a thing. Damian loves it. He loves how smart it makes him appear—that he's fooling the entire world. We're hidden—but right out in the open. Safe as long as we stay right where we are. I've never lived anywhere else but in this hotel."

"But you've been other places, right? You've seen other places."

"No."

"What about a regular school?"

She shook her head. "No."

"Ever been skateboarding?"

"No."

"Eaten a pizza?"

"No."

Nick squinted and looked over at her. "But…like…that's not normal, Isabella. That's freaky. Pizza is . . . you just have

74

to trust me on this one. You definitely want to eat pizza. Maybe there's a spell to make pizzas materialize."

Isabella laughed, and they continued to float, when suddenly Sascha stood and started pacing back and forth, her claws making a scraping, tapping sound on the tiles. Isabella and Nick each sat up.

"What's wrong, Sascha?" Isabella asked. Now the three polar bears began acting agitated, low growls rumbling in their throats, sounding like outboard motors.

Nick's heart beat a little faster. Sure, the polar bears seemed tame, but what if whatever magic spell Isabella cast on them stopped working, and he was about to be eaten alive by a very hungry polar bear?

Sascha roared—a full roar, no mere growl—and it echoed off the canyon-like walls of the indoor pool. From beneath the door, fingers of black, inky smoke extended, turning oily as the darkness seeped onto the floor. Sascha reared up on her legs as Nick heard Isabella hyperventilating next to him.

"What is it?"

"It's a Shadowkeeper, Nick. I've only seen one in the crystal ball. Never in real life. We're trapped!"

The oil spread across the entire floor, coating everything in thick, slick grease that Nick thought smelled like death. Not that he had ever smelled death before, but he was certain, if he ever did, it would be just like the overpowering scent filling the room. Nick's throat went dry. Now he realized it was the same scent on his floor at the Pendragon on the last day of school. It was also the scent from the cafeteria that same day.

The oils started to pool together again in one spot, and rose, forming what looked like a human. Nick gripped his polar bear, who was roaring as loud and bone-chillingly as Sascha.

Nick had never felt so cold and terrified in his life. The creature forming from the oil now sprouted leather-like wings, but its face was haggard and lined. It was human—and yet not. Its nose hooked like a shriveled carrot, and its fingers and toes were long, with nails like talons.

Nick looked over at Isabella. She had slid off her polar bear and was treading water. Her bear now climbed from the water and charged the creature, which emitted a sound like a high-pitched hiss. Isabella's bear rose up and swatted at the creature with its paws. With one flick of its wing, the creature sent the polar bear sailing against the floor with a horrifying cry of pain.

"Isabella? What do we do?" Nick whispered, but the creature looked right at him, its eyes an eerie blue color, like his own eyes, but…icier somehow, like they were dead, belonging to a corpse.

Isabella swam away until she was backed up against the wall of the pool. Nick saw her look desperately at the ladder.

There was no way they could climb out and get across the floor to the door after seeing what this thing had done to the polar bear.

Before he had time to think of a plan, his polar bear wrapped his massive body around him. He felt the muscles in his legs and the sharpness of his claws. The bear enveloped him until he couldn't even see. Nick let out a scream as the animal dove underwater. He took water into his lungs, and felt an agonizing need for air. He struggled against the beast as he dove deeper to the pool bottom. All Nick could see was water and fur and blackness.

They rose to the surface and he spat out water, choking and coughing before they dove again. He heard a loud sound as the creature plunged into the pool and the bear wrapped tighter around him, like a boa constrictor coiling around its prey.

With his hands, Nick beat against the chest of the bear, fighting for air, feeling the icy water up his nose and in his mouth.

The bear squeezed tighter still.

And then Nick's world went completely and utterly dark.

SOME ANSWERS
AND A RETURN

*H*E'S WAKING UP! SLAP HIM ON THE BACK!"
From somewhere, like being down a long tunnel, Nick heard voices. His eyelids fluttered, and he had the sudden urge to throw up. Sputtering and coughing, he felt someone turn him on his side and pound his back. Then he heard Isabella's voice. "It's okay, Nick. You're safe now."

He opened his eyes and saw Irina, Theo, and Isabella, as well as other members of the clan, staring down at him.

"Kolya…" Irina reached down and touched his cheek. "Are you all right?"

He nodded. Then shivered. His teeth chattered.

"Blankets!" Theo called out. He knelt down and helped Nick to a sitting position as someone wrapped a thick fur blanket around Nick's shoulders.

"What...happened?" Nick tried to think back, but all he remembered was the bear diving underwater with him.

The indoor pool area was now brightly lit up. Nick saw several men beside two of the bears, which lay sprawled on the tile, near the deep end of the pool. Their plush white fur was tinged pink with blood. The third bear was pacing near them, clearly agitated.

"Are they...?" He didn't even want to think it.

"No, they're not dead. But they are injured. If Sascha hadn't helped even the odds, I don't know that any of you would have survived," Theo said softly. He mussed Nick's wet hair.

Isabella's face was pale, and her lips trembled. "The Shadowkeeper didn't even look at me, Nick. It went right to you. If Mischa hadn't protected you like that..." She shuddered.

"So...so the bear wasn't trying to drown me?"

"*Drown* you? No!" Isabella said. "He was trying to *save* you."

"What were you two doing in here?" Theo demanded.

"It was my idea, Theo," said Isabella. "I thought Nick would like swimming with the bears. I've gone swimming with them before."

"But not at night. You cannot be in here alone. It's not safe anymore."

"I don't understand. Safe? The Winter Palace has always been safe for us." Isabella's voice was tremulous, and Nick worried she would start crying. He hated when girls cried.

Theo sighed. "Not anymore. Come on." Theo offered Nick his hand to help him stand up. "You need to see something." Leading the way, he and Irina left the pool area. Nick and Isabella followed them, dripping water on the carpet.

"We are in *so* much trouble," Isabella whispered.

"Yes, you are," Irina said over her shoulder. "But thank goodness we got there when we did."

"What happened to the creature?" Nick asked.

"Vanished."

A rock of dread sank heavy in Nick's gut. He would have felt a lot better if they had captured the creature, whatever it was.

Theo commanded a heavy door at the end of the hallway to open. It swung wide, though it looked like it was made of pure steel. Inside, banks of computers lined the walls along with dozens and dozens of monitors from security cameras. Members of the clan were pointing at different screens. A large tiger stood guard by the door, its eyes fierce. It stared at Nick as he entered.

Someone pointed at a monitor. "There! See him?"

Nick struggled to see, but the adults blocked his view. One or two of the security men turned around and parted for him and Isabella.

"I'm Zoltan," said the biggest, burliest—and hairiest—of the men. "I'm the Security Chief. We're like any other casino." He pressed buttons and close-ups of gambling tables appeared on some of the monitors. Nick saw dealers passing out cards at blackjack tables, and chips on green felt. "We watch for cheaters. Like him," he pointed at one screen. "He's trying to palm chips. We'll take care of him. And this one." He nodded toward a monitor where a woman in an evening gown played blackjack. "She's a card counter."

Nick stepped closer to the monitors.

"And here…the Shadowkeepers."

Nick felt his throat go dry—which was beyond strange, since he felt so waterlogged that he wondered if he'd ever feel dry and warm again. On the screen, he saw black shadows, like the creature with leatherlike wings, slipping between people unnoticed, as if the shadows were invisible.

"How are they not seeing those things?" he asked incredulously. They were right there.

"Humans, Nicholai," Zoltan said, "see what they want to see. They would rather be afraid of the stock market falling, of not getting the job they want, of silly horror movies than really open their eyes. Plus," he cleared his throat, "the Shadowkeepers have powerful magic."

"As powerful as ours?"

The adults exchanged glances, which Nick knew meant they just didn't want to tell him the bad news.

"Well," Zoltan said. "The balance between good and evil—"

Theo interrupted. "They are powerful, yes, Kolya. And they know you are here. They have never, since we immigrated to America, been this bold."

"That's not true," Irina said. Then she bit her lip.

Theo glared at her.

"They know *I'm* here? What do I have to do with anything?"

The room fell silent.

"Come on," Irina said. "It's time to get you two up to bed. It's late."

Nick started to ask Irina something, but he could see tears in her eyes, so he changed his mind. He was in enough trouble. He followed down the hall dejectedly, the blanket dragging behind him. Irina kept rubbing at her eyes. He wanted to know what was wrong, but he was tired. And now that he had time to think about it, his ribs hurt.

Irina opened the door to Isabella's room with a command. She said a few more words in Russian and the light switched on, the bedspread folded down, a drawer opened, and pajamas floated to the bed like clothes hanging on a clothesline on a breezy summer day.

"Take a shower, and then get some sleep," Irina said, hugging Isabella and giving her a peck on each cheek.

"What about Sascha?"

"We're bandaging her injured paw, but then she'll sleep here to keep an eye on you."

Isabella gave Nick a halfhearted wave good night. Down the hall, Nick opened his room. Irina swept in and checked in the closets and under the bed. He was going to tell her he hadn't checked under the bed since he was seven. But then again, after seeing that thing in the pool, maybe checking under the bed was a good idea.

When Irina was sure there was no one in the room, he expected her to say good night. Instead, she faced him.

"Your mother left the clan because she thought she would be safer without us. She thought if she was on her own, she could hide. I cried for months, every night, missing her. We had been girlhood best friends. We told each other all the secrets in our hearts. But she was convinced that away from us, they wouldn't find you."

"I don't understand."

"The Shadowkeepers live for one purpose. To destroy us. If they can capture our magic, it will make them more powerful. Our line is the most pure, the most powerful—and they know it. They want more of our power."

"How can they capture it?" Nick looked over at the empty cage where his hedgehog was *supposed* to be. If magic was so easy to capture, he'd be able to do it.

"When our clan left Russia, it was a time of panic and confusion. The communists were destroying *everything*. Libraries and art museums. Palaces. Buildings. They murdered many, many people. So our ancestors left—in a hurry, like everyone else. Like all refugees. Alone, cold, forgotten. And along the way, through sorcery and trickery, through thievery and *murder*, we lost some of our relics. Magic talismans that bring power to those who possess them. We've been battling to recover them ever since."

"So what does that have to do with me?"

"When your grandfather took you to Madame B.'s, it confirmed something."

"You knew I went there?"

She nodded. "You are a Gazer. You have the ability to see the past, to see the present, and to see the future. That gift comes along rarely. Your mother's side was powerful. The Shadowkeepers believe you must have the talismans. That your mother gave them to you, or at least that she left you something that points the way to them."

Nick shook his head and then thought of the key his grandfather had given him.

"What is it?" Irina asked.

"Nothing."

"Are you certain?"

He nodded.

"All right then, Nick. Know this—your mother was from the purest line of magician in the clan. She had no brothers or sisters and only one child. You represent, on your mother's side, our future."

"Does that mean those creatures are going to keep trying to kill me? Forever?"

Irina turned. "Those creatures just follow the bidding of the one who imprisons them. I'm afraid the real power of the Shawdowkeepers is far darker. But try not to worry."

"Easy for you to say," Nick whispered under his breath. They hadn't tried to drown her. Hadn't sprouted wings right in front of her eyes.

"Good night."

"'Night…Oh, one more thing."

"Yes?"

"When can I see my grandfather and father?"

"We can send for them. But remember, Kolya, the less your father knows, the safer he will be. Damian wants what goes on here to remain with the clan alone. He doesn't trust anyone outside the clan."

Nick stared at her. The way she said Damian's name, he couldn't decide if she was afraid of him or admired him.

Irina left, shutting the door behind her. Nick stripped out of his wet suit. Sure enough, where his ribs hurt there was an ugly, reddish-blue bruise forming. He padded into the bathroom, took the longest, hottest shower of his life, and changed into his sweats and Death Note T-shirt. He climbed into bed and sat there, thinking about the night.

And the more he thought about it, the angrier he got. That creature could have killed him. It could have killed Isabella, who was, about now, the only friend he had. A real friend who wasn't going off to Belize or who knows where else tomorrow. He shut his eyes, feeling a fury rising up in him. It was that feeling—not quite anger, not quite sadness, but... power. It was what Theo described.

Nick pictured the cage. The empty cage where he had somehow lost his hedgehog in space. He sat for a while, squeezing his eyes shut and concentrating on this electricity running through him, this feeling that started there, in the pit of his stomach. He imagined the feeling forming into a ball of electricity, with a glowing white-hot fury. He said the words Theo taught him. Whispered them, actually.

"*Krax pex phax.*"

And then he heard it. A faint rustling noise.

He looked up, and it was there. The hedgehog.

Nick leaped from bed and ran to the dresser. "I did it!" He leaned in close to the little spiny pet inside the gilded cage. "Sorry I lost you for a while, Vladimir."

Vladimir looked up at Nick with beady eyes. The hedgehog

waved a paw at him—like he totally understood what Nick had said. Then Vladimir shuffled off to the corner of the cage, curled into a ball, yawned, and went to sleep.

"Sleep sounds good to me, too," Nick yawned in reply.

He climbed back in bed, the last of his chills chased off by the soft, warm blankets, and sleep came over him like a heavy curtain.

✿　✿　✿

Something was burning him.

Nick bolted upright in bed and flicked on the light. His chest hurt. He pulled off his T-shirt and realized it was the key. It was hot. He touched it, and his fingertips burned, like touching a flame. He looked down at his chest. There, burned onto his skin, was a faint red imprint of the key.

"Am I dreaming?" But he knew he wasn't. It was hot. It was real.

The key was trying to tell him something. He was certain of it.

"What?" he asked it.

The key throbbed feverishly.

"What?" he asked it again, pleading this time.

But as quickly as it had heated to a molten-like burn, the key turned icy cold, pressed against his chest like a hunk of metal, as though it had never tried to communicate with him.

The key had to open something. Maybe something the Shawdowkeepers wanted. But what?

He thought hard. His father had a small safe in his closet where he kept their passports and some important papers—but he knew there was nothing valuable. He had been next to his father when he'd opened it. No secret jewels. Certainly no magic talismans. And the key to his dad's safe didn't look anything like this one. For one thing, the key around his neck looked ancient.

For another, the lettering was foreign. He needed to know what it said, but if he asked anyone in the clan to help him read it, then they would know he had it. And for some reason, he thought it would be better to keep it a secret for now. He didn't know how much to trust any of them.

Then Nick thought of the library where Damian had first taken him. Surely somewhere in that library was a book that would tell him what the letters said.

Nick lay back down and touched the key. His mother must have kept secrets from the clan. She definitely kept them from his dad. It was up to him to figure out those secrets. Before the Shadowkeepers did.

A PAIR OF VAULTS

*T*HE NEXT MORNING, NICK DECIDED THAT NO MATTER what was served—even fish eggs—he was eating breakfast. He dressed in a pair of black pants and a white shirt from his closet. He hated the feeling of the cuffs around his wrists, so he unbuttoned them and pushed the sleeves up. He looked like a waiter. He just wanted his old clothes.

While brushing his teeth, he saw in the mirror just how much he looked like Damian. Sure, maybe Damian thought making Nick part of the show was smart. But he wasn't Damian, no matter how much his hair color and eyes resembled his older cousin's.

He opened the door to his room and jumped backward. Two huge tigers—even bigger than Sascha—guarded his room. One lay like a furry doormat across the doorway.

The other paced back and forth in the hall like a sentinel, agitated.

At the sight of Nick, the tiger across the doorway stood up and then moved out of the way. The pacing tiger nodded, as if she was greeting him.

Nick nodded back, then walked down the hall to the family dining room. Behind him, he could hear the tigers following, and he felt a little like a wild boar in the grasslands, waiting to be their next meal. When he entered the dining room, the clan hushed. Isabella was there, sitting next to the Grand Duchess.

Nick looked at the food on the table and was grateful to see something other than caviar. He saw strawberries and cream in silver dishes, and something that looked like oatmeal. And there was also something that resembled Danish pastry—as long as it wasn't filled with cabbage, he figured he was all set.

Stomach growling, he filled a blue and gold rimmed plate with food and walked down to Isabella and the Grand Duchess. The old woman was wearing a long, old-fashioned dress with a high lace collar with ruffles. At her neck was pinned an enormous diamond and ruby brooch that glittered under the chandelier's lights.

Isabella's eyes seemed to ask him if he was okay, and he nodded and dug into his meal. He ate without saying a word until his plate was clean. Then the Grand Duchess whispered, "When I was a little girl, I believed the world was a beautiful place."

Nick looked over at her. The Grand Duchess's eyes were closed, and she rested her fingertips at the point of her chin.

"I lived in a palace filled with diamonds and jewels." She fingered the brooch at her neck. "We ate on plates rimmed with gold."

Nick looked down at his plate. A crest was etched in gold in the center of it. Surely, it couldn't be from the Grand Duchess's childhood.

"I played at the summer palace. The winter palace. My room," she clasped her hands together. "Filled with toys. Dolls in extravagant dresses, and a dollhouse filled with furniture carved by master craftsmen."

Nick couldn't move—he was afraid of disturbing her. He leaned forward, listening to her soft voice, wondering what secrets she would tell. The key felt warm against his chest.

"And then, I discovered that there will always be people, Kolya, full of deception. The man who deceived my parents still lives in a shadowy realm. He is cunning. Secretive. Powerful. And he...he is looking for something. He will not rest until he finds it." Though she looked half-asleep, she suddenly opened her eyes and stared knowingly at him.

The key burned hotter, and it was all Nick could do to keep from yelping. He was about to ask the Grand Duchess more about this man when Theo entered the room.

"Kolya, time for school."

Nick looked at Isabella. She shook her head and whispered, "I'm working with Irina today. Just you."

Nick stood and walked to Theo, following him out of the dining room and toward the classroom. Once in there, Theo handed him a crystal ball and a small pedestal for it to rest on and then gestured for Nick to sit at his desk.

"This ball is yours—it was your great-grandmother's. You get to keep this one. After last night, your training is being accelerated. The first rule of the ball is you must approach with a pure heart or it will deceive you."

"The rule of the ball?" Nick rolled his eyes. Everyone in the family was so dramatic. "What does that even mean?"

Theo looked at his watch. "Ask your ball for the number the roulette wheel at table eighty-five will land on in ten minutes."

Nick looked at Theo. "Ask the ball? Like talk to it?"

"Exactly."

"I feel like an idiot talking to a ball."

"Put your hand on the ball. It's yours. You must bond with it."

"Bond?"

"Just do as I say."

"All right." Nick rubbed his hands on the crystal ball. It felt warm to his touch—alive in a way. But he knew that was impossible. Feeling foolish, he said, "Crystal ball, what number will the roulette ball land on in ten minutes at table eighty-five?"

The ball filled with a smoky green haze, and then Nick saw, in a flash—twelve red.

Nick smiled at Theo. "It gave me the number!"

Theo smiled at him, sat down at his desk, and said a few words, and a pot of tea appeared. "We wait. Care for tea?"

"No. Why can't you guys drink soda?"

"It's not our way."

Nick rolled his eyes again and leaned back in his chair. If he had a crystal ball that told him numbers to bet on, that could predict the future, then he would be rich. No more small hotels with his dad. Heck, they could *buy* a hotel. A hotel where he would serve cheeseburgers and orange soda and pizza, and he wouldn't have to wear ridiculous black pants and white shirts. He'd ride his skateboard through the halls, and there'd be a skateboard ramp in the lobby.

After about ten minutes, Theo took his own ball and spoke to it, and Nick could see inside the casino. Theo spoke in Russian, and a roulette wheel appeared close up. The dealer spun the wheel. It whirred. The little ball flung around, click, click, click…and landed on eight black.

Nick looked at Theo, puzzled. "What happened? Why wasn't it twelve red?"

"Precisely what I said. You must approach your crystal ball with a pure heart. It will deceive you otherwise."

"But how do I know if I have a pure heart?"

"You cannot ask for personal gain. You must ask with the intention of doing good. Not for money or fame or riches. You must learn to discern, my young cousin. And most importantly, you must learn to do it quickly. The Shadowkeepers are closing in."

"How long have you been reading crystal balls?"

"Since I was your age."

"Well, how can I ever get good at it so fast? I need more time."

"The Shadowkeepers do not care about such things."

"But what do they want?"

Even as Nick asked, the key burned.

"Come," Theo said. He stood and led Nick out of the classroom and down the hall to an elevator. The minute Theo stood in front of it, the doors opened. Nick jumped back. An enormous brown bear took up most of the car.

"Our elevator operator. Keeps out the riffraff."

They stepped onto the elevator, and Nick noticed there were no buttons at all on the elevator's panel. The doors closed, and with a whoosh that made his stomach feel like it dropped to his shoes, they descended.

"Where are we going?" Nick asked, aware that the bear's breath was hot near his neck.

"The vault."

The doors opened, and as they exited the elevator, they entered an enormous room. The floors were marble, and their heels clicked on them as they walked. The ceilings were three stories high, Nick guessed. Like Damian's library, they were painted with scenes of magic in Russia, fanciful pictures of people flying through the air and polar bears and tigers soaring over onion-topped domes in snow-covered Siberia. As he looked upward, the pictures moved, stars twinkled, and occasionally a polar bear dove into a painted water scene.

"This is the vault," Theo swept his hand to the left, "that we show the Nevada Gaming Commission if they come to check out our casino."

Nick looked and saw a bank of security cameras and a command center with lights flashing and occasionally beeping.

"If someone broke in, would alarms go off?"

"I don't know. No one's ever tried. Those lights and beeps are just magic—for show." Theo pressed a button. Inside the vault, a camera zoomed in on money. Piles and piles of money.

"Whoa!" Nick said, leaning in close to the monitor. "Look at all that. It must be…what? Millions? Billions? Zillions?"

"It's just money." Theo walked on, but stacks of hundred-dollar bills mesmerized Nick, and they rose as high as the wall. There were also sacks of what he guessed was more money and coins. More money than he could ever spend or even imagine, though he wouldn't mind trying to spend it. Sure beat his five-dollar-a-week allowance.

"This," Theo gestured to a wall, "is our real vault."

Nick stared. "It's a wall." He stepped over to it and ran his hand along it. The wall was cool cement, stories high.

"Maybe." Theo walked over to the wall and stepped through it. One second, he was there—and the next, he was gone. "Come on," he called out from behind the wall.

"How?"

"Believe."

"Yeah, right." Nick pressed his hands along the wall and shook his head. It was solid cement. He moved to the spot where Theo walked through. It was just as solid as the rest of the wall.

"Come on!" Theo shouted. "Believe, Kolya!"

Nick shut his eyes. Suddenly, he felt cool air on his face. Without opening his eyes, he touched the wall again and his hand shot through! Taking a deep breath, he stepped through. It was like walking through a wind tunnel, and as his foot reached the other side, a strange gust of magic whipped through his hair, standing it up on end, like static electricity. He joined Theo in an even bigger vault that looked like a museum. Glass cases lined every wall—ten feet high around the room.

"This is our most valuable collection. This is what we do, as Magickeepers. We are collectors."

"What do you collect?"

"Come." Theo led Nick to each case—hundreds of them. Each one had a small brass plaque—just like in a museum—denoting its significance and sometimes the donor.

Nick read the first plaque. "Sword of Life, recovered from the tomb of King Tut by Howard Carter. Donated by Howard Carter after the death of Lord Carnarvon."

"This relic is from the Curse of the Pharaohs. Howard Carter was a minor Magickeeper. Weak bloodline—nothing like ours."

"What's this death of Lord Carnarvon?"

"After the tomb of King Tut was discovered and disturbed, Lord Carnarvon died in a freak shaving accident."

"Freak shaving accident?"

"Blood poisoning. Got into a nick he sustained while shaving. Howard Carter became frightened and smuggled the Sword of Life out from the tomb. He donated it to the family vault so that it would prevent any further deaths—and so it didn't fall into the hands of any Shadowkeepers."

"What is the Sword of Life?"

"There were two Swords of Life created in the forges of the Pharaohs. This one is safe in the vault. Damian uses the other in the show. You can pierce a person all the way through and not kill them. It's the most masterful of illusions. Utter a different spell, and a soldier using it in battle is unable to be defeated. For obvious reasons, we would not want this falling into the wrong hands."

The brilliant silver sword gleamed beneath the lights of the glass case. Gold wrapped around its hilt in the shape of a serpent's head. Jewels glittered on the hilt, including a diamond the size of a robin's egg. Emeralds gleamed for the serpent's eyes.

Nick walked to the next case. "This is nothing but a bunch of rocks."

"Read the plaque."

"Stones of Strength. Discovered by Igor Kashin, 1402. Recovered from the Shadowkeepers by Mikhail Kirov, who died in the valiant effort."

Theo clapped a hand on Nick's shoulder. "Poor Mikhail."

"What are Stones of Strength?"

"Have you ever heard of Stonehenge?"

"That place with the huge stones in England?"

"And my brother said you were awful at social studies. Yes, that place with the huge stones. Some of them weigh fifty tons. And yet, how did they get there?"

Nick shrugged.

"They didn't have machines back in 3000 BC. Even with powerful machines, how indeed would they be moved?"

He pointed in the case at the small rocks. "The Stones of Strength. You place them in a formation, cast a spell, and they can move rocks many hundreds times their weight. Can you imagine? In the hands of a Shadowkeeper, they could be dropped on a building! A whole town could be destroyed. Hence, far safer in our vault."

They moved several cases down, and Nick's eyes widened. "Fabergé egg belonging to Tatyana Petrov, donated after her death, for safekeeping." He looked up at Theo. "This was my mother's?"

"Yes. And it is yours. But we keep it safe here for now."

"What magic does it do?"

"This one is less about magic and more about our history. We had a relationship with the Fabergé family stretching back to the Tsar. Very few of these imperial eggs survived."

"It's beautiful," Nick said. The egg was large and ornate, gilded and encrusted with gems. It had to be worth a fortune.

Nick and Theo kept walking until they came to dozens of empty cases. "What are these? Invisible things?"

Theo laughed. "No. These are cases waiting for relics lost to us. Like the Eternal Hourglass. We have the pocket watch you saw in the crystal ball, but the Eternal Hourglass eludes us. And that case there is for the Chalice of Immortality. And over there, the Dagger of Mayhem. You don't even want to know what that can do."

"So, no offense, Theo, but I found that hole in the vault wall pretty easily—I mean, after you walked through. If all this stuff is so valuable, aren't you worried someone—or something—will break in and steal it all? Just walk through?"

"No. That hole was there because I cast the spell. It will be gone when we leave. And the traditional entrance is booby-trapped. Damian designed the traps himself. Everything from a Floor of Death to ravenous Siberian tigers to a Door of Deception."

"So no one's ever tried to steal the relics?"

Theo shook his head. "No. Well, there was one time, but the tigers had a lovely meal. But I put nothing past the Shadowkeepers. They came here for something. We just need to find out what. Then we can defeat them."

Again, the key burned against Nick's chest. He wanted to tell Theo about it, but he wasn't yet sure what to make of his newfound family. He still half-expected a bear or tiger to eat him. What kind of family kept man-eating pets?

A HORSE OF GOLD

*T*HAT AFTERNOON, THEO AND NICK WORKED ON LEARNING the Russian alphabet.

"Can't you people just have regular letters?"

"Can't the rest of the world accept how much better our way is?" Theo asked.

"I'll never learn this. It gives me a headache."

"Study it and you will learn."

Nick bent his head over the book. The letters swam in front of him. Then Damian entered the room.

"Cousin!"

Nick looked up.

"I heard about last night."

Nick expected some sympathy—after all, he'd nearly drowned. But no sympathy was forthcoming.

"There is no time for licking your wounds. Come! Your horse awaits."

So much for giving him a break. Nick groaned inwardly. Learn the Russian alphabet, or climb on a horse? Neither choice appealed to him. He shut his book and reluctantly followed Damian out into the hallway.

"I'm really tired, Damian. Maybe today isn't the best day to try to learn to ride, to be in the show."

"Nonsense. Every day is a day for magic. Come along."

Nick glared at his cousin. Something about Damian bothered him—Damian thought he was always right.

They rode down in an elevator. Damian didn't ask him a single question about the creature from the night before, about nearly drowning. Didn't he care? When the doors opened with a near-silent whoosh, they walked down a long hallway in what Nick guessed was the basement of the massive casino. The walls were cement, the floors were cement, and their footfalls echoed, especially Damian's, because he wore black polished boots. Pipes were strung along the ceiling, and Nick heard the hissing sound of steam and water carried along the pipes.

At the end of the hallway, Damian pressed a button, and they rode up another elevator.

"So why don't you just magically teleport us or whatever it is you do? Why walk? You're the 'all-powerful' Damian, after all." Nick glared at his cousin.

"If you're trying to be an ungrateful little brat, you are succeeding."

"Ungrateful? Let's see...you kidnapped me on my thirteenth birthday, and within forty-eight hours, I practically drowned. The entire time I lived with my dad, no one ever tried to kill me."

"Oh, really?" Damian arched an eyebrow. "You're so sure about that?"

"Yeah, I am."

Something about how Damian asked him made Nick doubt all of a sudden. More secrets. Nick couldn't wait to see his grandfather again and ask him everything he'd been hiding all these years.

When the elevator doors opened again, they were backstage, which bustled with activity and animals rehearsing.

Nick's mouth dropped open in amazement. He didn't realize just how many people worked on a show like Damian's. There had to have been a hundred—some in costume, some clad in black like stagehands.

Nick peered out at the theater seats. He knew from the television commercials that the Winter Palace Theatre seated 4,200 people—and there wasn't a bad seat in the house, according to the critics. Even with a theater that seated so many, the waiting time for tickets was measured in months and years, not days or weeks.

In the center of the immense stage stood the most beautiful horse he had ever seen. It gleamed as if its coat were really made of gold. And it was huge. Nearly twice as tall as Nick. Next to it stood the crazy horse trader he had seen in the crystal ball. The horse was snorting wildly, straining against its bridle, and lifting its front hooves off the ground in protest. Great. They got him a majestic but wild horse.

"Here's what will happen," Damian said. He pointed to a spot so far off at the back of the theater that Nick had to squint to actually see it. "Nick, you will sit astride your magnificent horse and will rise up from a trapdoor in the floor over there, charge full speed down a special catwalk, jump over a huge snowbank configured to look like a glacier, dismount on the ice, fight two tigers, then cast a spell, changing Sascha into Isabella. They'll switch places. Then you and Isabella will take a bow. Then…you're done. Curtain drops."

Nick started laughing—howling actually. "You have got to be kidding me."

Damian looked at him sternly. "I never kid."

"I can tell."

Damian narrowed his eyes even more. "It will be brilliant. You will be brilliant. I insist."

"First of all, you're not getting me on that crazy horse. Second, if I ever got on the horse, maybe I would make it walk, but I sure as heck am not going to ride it full charge down a gangplank or whatever you want to call it. Then… how do you propose I switch Isabella with Sascha? I'm just getting the hang of moving around a hedgehog."

Damian stamped his foot. "That's my little brother Theo's way of babying you. Why start with a hedgehog? Start with a *tiger*. It's all the same magic anyway." He snapped his finger in the air and stamped his foot again.

Nick couldn't believe Damian talked about Theo that way. "It's easy for you, maybe. But in case you forgot, I just got here. Maybe you should have kidnapped me a while ago if it's so important to put me in your show! I'm new at this."

"Doesn't matter." Damian waved his hand. "Up on the horse then. Rehearsal. You have to do this perfectly in two weeks. Opening night. For the summer tourists." He rolled his eyes. "They think we have the best show on the strip. Like some Disneyland trickery. No one suspects that they are actually seeing the world's most incredible magicians at work. They do not appreciate the art."

Nick crossed his arms. "I'm not getting on the horse."

As if it had read Nick's mind, the horse reared up, causing Sergei the horse trader to command, "Come on, you crazy beast. Settle down!"

Damian walked behind Nick and gave him a little push. "Let's go, Nicholai. You have two weeks to learn this. Two weeks before opening night."

Nick wheeled around on his heels. "Wait a minute. How did you know I was even going to be in the show?"

Damian started walking away, his black boots echoing on the wooden stage. Nick ran after him and grabbed his shirt.

"Tell me! You have the horse, the show, the whole thing planned. How did you know I was coming here? How long have you been planning this?"

The key against his chest burned again. He expected Damian to yell at him, but instead he pulled Nick very close, lowering his voice to a whisper.

"Since you were a baby, we all knew one day you'd come back to us. But this birthday...this birthday meant it was time, Kolya. Now, you are my cousin, but you also are my *apprentice*. Get...on...that...horse."

He said the last words so tersely, that Nick could see Damian's jaw clenching.

"Fine!" Nick whipped himself away from Damian, who had draped an arm across Nick's shoulder, and marched over to the horse.

Sergei had watched the two of them, his face pale. "You do not want to get Damian angry," he whispered.

Nick looked over his shoulder, right at Damian. "I don't care."

"It is a serious mistake, my little friend."

"He's being a jerk."

"Listen," Sergei whispered. "He turned my fourth cousin into a pig. Eventually, he turned him back, but he still oinks sometimes. Just don't cross him."

Nick turned back to look up at the horse. Up close, it was even more magnificent. Its coat gleamed as if Sergei had brushed it a thousand times, ten thousand times, before bringing it to the theater. Nick touched the horse's side, the muscles rippling, alive, strong.

"Fine. What's the horse's name?"

"Maslow."

"Hey, Maslow," Nick whispered. The horse startled again, rising up on his hind legs. Nick's heart pounded. He had never been on a pony ride, let alone a horse like this.

The entire theater of performers—all the family—stared at him and the horse. He moved closer to the horse. "Come on, Maslow," Nick said softly. He touched the saddle and the horse bucked insanely, his black eyes wild, looking frightened, deranged even.

Damian stormed toward Sergei. "Has this horse been broken properly? And don't lie to me."

"Well..." Sergei turned his palms upward. "You wanted an Akhal-Teke. They are wild, Damian. You know that. They are not like any other horse in the world."

"Leave him to me!" a woman's voice rang out.

Across the stage, Irina strode, chin high and haughty. Nick

held his breath. She walked like a dancer, long legs striding gracefully, like she was floating. Nick looked over at Damian, and saw that he was flushed. Damian—*the* Damian—was mesmerized by her. His cousin stared at Irina.

Her heels clicked on the stage. She reached Maslow and patted the horse on his neck. Then she took the reins and pulled the horse's head ever so slightly toward her, forcing it to bend. She whispered in the horse's ear in Russian. Nick had no idea what she was saying, but her voice was commanding and powerful. She continued to speak to the horse. When she was done, she released the reins with a flourish and clapped her hands three times. She looked over at Damian, a satisfied expression on her face.

"There is always the easy way around these problems," she murmured. "And *your* way."

She took Nick's hand. "Maslow will listen to you now. He will never harm you and will protect you—to the death."

Nick thought of the polar bears. He hoped it never came to that point.

"Come on." She led him to the horse and helped him mount the Akhal-Teke. She placed the reins in his hands.

"You just have to *think* about where you want to go now. Don't worry about the reins so much. *Will* the horse where you want him to go. Become *one* with him. He will listen now."

Nick nodded. The ground looked a long…long…long way down. The horse twitched, and he could feel his power. He took the reins and figured he might as well aim for the far corner of the theater. He shut his eyes for a moment, as he did when he tried to conjure up his hedgehog. Nothing happened. So he took a deep breath. He forgot about Irina and Isabella, about the polar bears and the Shadowkeepers. He forgot about Damian. He most especially forgot that his cousin wanted him to perform in front of thousands of people in two weeks.

And a funny thing happened. He felt the horse move. Then he could hear the clip, clip, clopping on the wooden floor. Maslow picked up speed. Nick opened his eyes and saw that Maslow was galloping across the theater, the hot lights and the red velvet seats just a blur. He had never moved so fast before—except on a roller coaster. He held on, terrified of falling, but also feeling as one with the horse. Finally, with a last leap, the horse landed precisely on the spot where Damian told him. Nick was breathless, and he felt the horse's sides heaving in and out. Nick leaned down to pat his horse's neck.

Down on the stage, he saw what he thought was the faintest of smiles cross Damian's mouth. His cousin crossed his arms.

Nick scratched behind the horse's ears as it whinnied softly. "Attaboy, Maslow," he said. "We'll show Damian yet."

GRANDPA'S TRIUMPHANT RETURN

*A*FTER HE HAD REHEARSED EVERYTHING BUT CHANGING Isabella into Sascha, and after he had done it a hundred times, until his legs were sore and his butt was numb in the saddle, Nick dismounted, his growling stomach reminding him it was time to eat.

He was about to head with the family to the elevators up to the top floor when, in the back of the theater, he saw his grandfather. Nick waved wildly and, sore legs aside, ran down the stage steps and up the aisle, bear-hugging his mother's father.

"Man, it's good to see you," he smiled at Grandpa.

His grandfather ruffled his hair and hugged him back fiercely, his voice choked off. "Good to see you, too."

Nick looked up at his grandfather. "Why didn't you tell me?"

"Come on, my boy," his grandfather said. "Let's go for a walk."

Nick nodded, glancing over his shoulder. He saw Damian staring at him. The heck with him. This was his grandfather.

The two of them strolled out into the lobby. Tourists were marveling at the snow-topped onion domes.

"How do they do it?" said one man with so many cameras slung around his neck, Nick was surprised he wasn't hunchbacked.

"I hear it's soap powder. Like Disney does," offered a woman, obviously his wife, with dyed red hair that matched the lobster red of her sunburned skin, and wearing a Hawaiian-themed dress with hula dancers on it.

Nick and Grandpa moved through the lobby. Nick looked all around for Shadowkeepers but didn't see any.

"They're not here, if that's what you're worried about," his grandfather said.

Nick's eyes widened. "You know about them?"

His grandfather nodded.

"What else do you know?"

The old man exhaled. "I know, Kolya, that you are better off here."

"How? How can I be better off here? Don't you miss me? Don't you *want* me? They have me riding some crazy horse, eating food that would make you throw up."

"That food is your heritage. But I did bring you something." His grandfather reached into his pocket and pulled out a fast-food cheeseburger, still warm, wrapped in brightly hued paper.

"All right!" Nick unwrapped it and took a huge bite, savoring the smell, the pickle, the ketchup—all of it. With a mouth full of cheeseburger, he tried to swallow as he kept talking. "Their food is gross. And I don't have a TV. I don't have video games. I don't have my skateboard. I don't have anything but this crazy family I didn't even know I had, who all talk in spells and riddles. And Russian! And last night, a Shadowkeeper tried to kill me, and I almost drowned."

As he said that, his ribs reminded him just how close he had come to drowning.

Grandpa looked at him, fear registering in his eyes. "They came here? They got past Damian's security?"

Nick nodded. "I'm not safe here."

"Kolya, you aren't safe anywhere else but here."

"But I don't understand."

"Come sit down."

Grandpa led him to a small velvet couch by a huge potted plant with blue flowers. Nick finished scarfing down his burger and crumpled the paper into a ball.

"These grow in Russia," Grandpa said, touching a bloom that hung like a bell off the vine of the plant.

"I didn't know you were from Russia. I mean, I knew like a long, long time ago that you were from somewhere else. But I didn't know any of this. Why didn't you tell me?"

"It was safer that way, Kolya. Your mother thought that if she married an ordinary human, if she changed her hair color, if she moved to an innocuous little Vegas hotel and worked as a magician's assistant, then no one would know where you were. She wanted to blend in among the ordinary. It didn't work. After she…died…a spell of protection was cast over you." Grandpa lowered his voice and leaned to whisper in Nick's ear. "Remember these words: *Oberezhnyj scheet predkov hranit menia.*"

As soon as Grandpa uttered the spell, the key warmed against Nick's chest and a hot breeze caressed his face. Suddenly, there was a flash in his mind, as if he was looking in a crystal ball—only his crystal ball was back in his room.

"What?" his grandfather asked.

Nick felt dizzy, and he reached his hands out to steady himself on the couch. He saw something so clearly that it was as if it stood there in front of him—only he knew it was in his mind.

"You see something, don't you?' Grandpa asked.

Nick nodded. "I saw something. I mean, it made no sense. I saw Damian. Younger. His hair was longer. And I saw Theo. And my mother was there. But it seemed so real."

"What has Theo taught you about ball gazing?"

"Just that I have to approach the ball with an open heart. A pure heart."

"But has he talked to you about being a Gazer? About the bloodline?"

Nick shook his head. "Not really."

"A powerful Gazer will have flashes from the ball even when the ball isn't there. What you saw—that was from your ball. Theo obviously chose your ball well."

"He said it was my great-grandmother's."

Grandpa started laughing.

"What's so funny?"

"Your great-grandmother was my mother-in-law, the old battle-ax. But she sure was powerful. It's a great ball. And it's communicating with you. And the more you use it, the more you understand its power, the stronger your abilities will become."

"How do you know all this?"

"I was once part of this family, too, Nick. But Damian and I had a disagreement, shall we say. Over a relic. And I decided to leave. Shortly afterward, your mother left, too. But now, I can see Damian was right, Nick. You are safer here."

"But if there was a spell of protection, how come they nearly killed me?"

"The spell was only protection until the year of your becoming a man."

"Eighteen?"

"No. Thirteen. And perhaps two days before your birthday, I saw a shadow cross over the sidewalk outside the Pendragon. I knew they would come for you, Kolya."

"So why don't we just…move? Go somewhere else? You used to tell me stories about New York. You loved New York. And what about San Francisco? I've never even seen the ocean."

His grandfather shook his head. "It's not so simple. I can't keep you safe. Your grandmother's lineage—that's Damian's—was more powerful than my own. And your father…" His grandfather looked down at his hands. "Much as he loves you, he can't keep you safe at all, Kolya."

"So I'm stuck here." He thought of Isabella never going to a regular school, never eating pizza, never knowing life outside the hotel. It felt like a prison, even though it was one of the most famous and glamorous places on earth.

"I'm afraid so."

Nick looked down. He unbuttoned his shirt and moved aside the key. A red imprint, like a bad sunburn, had formed the outline of the key against his chest. Nick swallowed hard. "What does this open, Grandpa? It's burning me."

"I don't know. The only thing I do know is she died protecting it."

"I thought she got sick, Grandpa."

His grandfather wiped at his eyes. "I can't talk about this. But it's up to you. Find out what that key unlocks, and maybe it can keep you safe from them." He shook his head. "In the meantime, Kolya, learn everything you can. The stronger a magician you are, the safer you'll be."

Nick shook his head, feeling a rock in his stomach. "But I can't. I'm not Damian. I'm not Theo. Grandpa, I made a hedgehog move. Big deal. Come on. Those Shadowkeepers… what chance do I ever have against them?"

"You have something they don't have."

"What?"

Grandpa stood. "You have the family, Nick."

From across the lobby, he saw his father walking toward him carrying a shopping bag.

"Why don't you and Dad stay here, too?"

His grandfather shook his head. "That's not a good idea, Nick. Not right now."

When his father reached them, he hugged Nick. "How are you?"

Nick looked up at his dad. His father used to seem so much taller—Nick's head always hit somewhere on his dad's chest when they hugged. Now, he could almost look him in the eyes. His father's eyes were rimmed red, and he was pale. Now he knew why his grandfather thought it best to keep things how they were—at least for now.

"I'm okay, Dad. I don't want you to worry. They are taking really good care of me, and except for the fact that there's no pizza and cheeseburgers, it's great." He tried to muster up all the fake enthusiasm he could, like when he used to tell his dad that his act at the Pendragon was awesome.

"You with no cheeseburgers? Come on." His dad winked at him.

"How come you didn't tell me about her?" Nick asked.

"I thought that maybe it would all just go away, Nick. That they would forget about you. Part of me didn't really understand. Not fully. All this talk of bloodlines, I thought it was just your grandfather being proud of your heritage. I thought it was just a lot of talk."

"Dad, it's all real. I wouldn't have believed it but…"

"Now I know why none of my tricks have worked since she died."

Nick struggled to think of something to say, something to make his dad less sad. "I promise to learn everything I can, Dad. Then…then I'll have a magic act. We can work together."

His father smiled slightly and put a hand on each of Nick's shoulders. "All right, then. One day, we'll work together. Now, look in the shopping bag. We never got to pick out your birthday present."

Nick grinned, hoping it was what he thought it was.

He ripped aside tissue paper, and sure enough, it was his dream skateboard, with a wider seven-ply deck and a skull and crossbones on it. "Thanks!" Nick said. He already imagined riding on it in the basement of the hotel.

"It's the one you wanted, right?"

"The exact one."

"Enjoy it, then. In the meantime, your mother used to have this Russian saying, 'Eat what is cooked; listen to what is said.'"

"What? So that's how she got through eating Russian food?"

His dad laughed. "I think so. But remember to listen. And stay safe. I'll come see you on opening night."

"How did you know?"

And then Nick saw it. Rising two stories high at the other end of the lobby was the poster for the new show. Damian, of course, was front and center, staring out over all who entered the hotel's opulent lobby. Next to him was a white tiger; on the other side, a huge polar bear. And behind Damian on the poster, stood a horse, a rider on its back.

A young Damian.

Nick.

ACCELERATED TRAINING

"REMEMBER HOW I SAID YOU WERE ON AN ACCELERATED training schedule?" Theo asked. He peered over his glasses as Nick painstakingly wrote the Cyrillic alphabet while his hedgehog looked on, bored.

"Yeah," Nick murmured.

"Good. Because you and Boris have *sword fighting* at one o'clock."

"Huh?" Nick looked up. "That's really funny, because I thought I heard you say sword fighting at one."

"I did. And look, it's one o'clock now." As if on cue, an enormous cuckoo clock's hands clicked to one o'clock. A door opened, and a strange-looking bird popped out and said, "One o'clock." It ruffled its feathers, which were ebony and shiny and gleamed with a purplish sheen, then preened them some more. Finally, it looked down from the wall and screeched, "Nick! It's one o'clock on the dot. Get moving!" It squawked once more and disappeared behind the doors of the clock again.

"All right!" Nick snapped. "Fine. I'll get going. But who's Boris?"

"I am," said a deep voice from the doorway, which seemed to be blocked, casting the room into dimness. Nick turned around, and there stood the biggest man he had ever seen, with layers of muscle on layers of muscle and a shiny bald head—with eyes the same color as his own. Make that eye. His left eye had a black eye patch over it like a pirate, and an angry scar ran down his face. Boris looked like he could crush Nick between his thumb and index finger.

"Great," Nick said. He glanced at Theo, stood, and followed Boris out into the hall. They walked down to the very far end, and Boris spoke to the door—this one heavy and wooden, like from some medieval dungeon. It swung open, and Nick found himself in a huge room with wooden floors covered in mats, and walls lined with strange costumes, swords, and plates of armor.

Boris gestured for Nick to stand in the middle of the room. He sized him up and then pointed at a sword. It flew across the room, its tip pointed right at Nick. He screamed and ducked. The sword fell clattering to the ground.

"Are you crazy?" Nick screamed. "No, make that, is *everyone* here crazy? Are they? You could have killed me."

"No. I am finding a sword for you. Hold still!" At that, Boris pulled Nick back up to a standing position. "Hold still. You think I would risk harming a hair on your head? This is the only way."

Boris began signaling at other swords, which flew toward Nick. They sliced through the air, making a faint whistling sound. Each one poised in the air, hovering, before crashing to the floor. Finally, only one sword remained on the wall. Boris gestured to it.

The sword flew through the air and circled Nick several times, before swooping down and placing its hilt gently into Nick's hand.

Nick held it up. The hilt was encrusted with three red rubies. "It's heavy," Nick observed.

"Sure. Of course. You expect it to be plastic?" Boris snorted. He raised his hands and all the other swords rose from the floor and flew back to their rightful places on the wall.

"Now, we fight."

Boris took off his white shirt, revealing a muscle shirt beneath that only served to show off his immense biceps. They looked like the boughs of a sturdy tree.

"You've got to be kidding me."

"No."

"You'll pulverize me."

Boris's sword flew to him from the wall, and Boris wrapped a thick, meaty hand around it. "We do not fight. Our swords do." Boris let go of his hilt and the sword stayed suspended in midair, almost gracefully, as if it were as light as a feather. Nick let go of his sword, and it crashed to the ground.

"No!" Boris said. "You must take this seriously."

Nick sighed. "You have shiny metal swords flying at me. You think I'm not going to take this seriously?"

"Concentrate. Close your eyes."

"If I close my eyes, how can I see where your sword is? How do I know you won't just chop my head off with one of these swords?"

"Silly young cousin, if I wanted to kill you, I already would have. You are like a little fly I can swat."

"That makes me feel *so* much better. We're cousins, too?"

"Yes."

Nick looked up at Boris. The scar ran down his face from beneath the eye patch almost to his neck. It was purplish and red, and it looked like whatever Boris's long-ago wound was, it was deep. Whoever got him with the sword...Nick shuddered to think of what was under that patch.

Boris snapped his fingers, and a black satin scarf appeared in his hand. "All right. You won't close your eyes, so we do it this way." He stood behind Nick and roughly blindfolded him.

With his eyes covered, Nick's mind flashed. He staggered back a foot or two, heart pounding. He could see the swords in his mind. Now he struggled to feel his sword. As if, somehow, he could stretch his hand, invisibly, to the hilt, and control it.

Nick could hear the two swords colliding in midair. He united with the sword in his mind, until he flashed on it being forged. He saw the sword's maker. He looked Japanese, wearing flowing white robes, with a Japanese-style house in the distance surrounded by cherry blossom trees.

Nick felt heat, as if he were next to the anvil and the fire. He was far away—and yet he was still in the room with Boris.

Boris untied his blindfold, but Nick didn't lose his concentration.

"You may look now," Boris said.

Nick opened his eyes. The swords were fighting in midair, striking each other with such intensity that sparks flew from their blades and fell to the ground.

Boris waved his hand, and the two swords separated. Nick's flew to his side.

Boris took the hilt of Nick's sword. "Give me your palm."

"Why?"

"This is your sword, Nicholai. It cannot harm you." He took the end of the sword and pressed it against the fleshy part of the heel of Nick's hand. Nothing happened. No cut. No blood.

But Nick knew the sword could slice through anything. It could find its mark, itst target. He didn't know how he knew, but he did.

"Wow."

"You take the sword. It will defend you. But just as Theo trains you with your crystal ball, the sword must be wielded with an open heart, never for personal gain, nor for simple revenge. Only to save your life or the lives of your loved ones if under attack. If not, the blade could cut you. Do you understand, Kolya?"

Nick nodded.

"Good."

Boris bowed to Nick.

Nick bowed back. He took his sword, which still emanated heat.

Okay, so there weren't cheeseburgers, he hated fish eggs, and Shadowkeepers wanted to kill him—but the sword stuff was cool.

A GREAT DEAL ON A DANCING BEAR!

BACK IN HIS ROOM, NICK LOOKED AROUND FOR SOMEPLACE to store his sword. As if it had read his mind, the sword flew from his hand to the wall, hanging there perfectly though nothing held it up but magic. Nick smiled. The sword made the last few days worth it. Almost.

His crystal ball sat on its pedestal on the dresser. Feeling silly, he did what Theo had taught him. He approached the ball and rubbed his hands on it, familiarizing himself with his crystal ball. Theo said it was how the ball would "imprint" on Nick. It was how relics and magic worked in their world. Objects bonded to the magicians they were destined to serve.

Suddenly, the ball grew hazy, filling with a bluish smoke. Nick waited for the smoke to clear away. He heard someone coughing, and Crazy Sergei appeared inside, waving his hands.

"Hey, Nick!" He coughed. "I hate the blue smoke." He coughed again. "Smells like pickled herring."

"What are you doing in my crystal ball?"

"You happy with your horse?"

Nick shrugged. "Yeah. I mean, now that Irina calmed him down. I could have been killed climbing on him at first. Between swords, the horse, and nearly drowning, so far being around you people has been pretty dangerous."

"But for a chance to learn Damian's secrets? It's the chance any Magickeeper in the entire world would kill for."

Nick gulped. Maybe that was what he feared. He didn't want to learn things magicians would kill for.

"Listen, I have a good deal on a brown bear. From circus. He already dances on a ball. Good trick. I think you will like him."

"I can't have a pet bear, Sergei. That's Isabella's area, not mine."

"But it's a *steal*. For you, cheap. He's very tame. He could be like roommate. Keep you company."

Nick shook his head. "Ask Damian."

"I can't. Damian hates me."

"But he bought my horse from you."

"Only because I am the last dealer of the Akhal-Teke. Please. Talk to him. The bear is adorable. Very smart. He can count to four. You say, 'Bear, count to four,' and it claps paws four times. Charming."

The image of Sergei was replaced by a brown bear dancing on a red ball in a Russian circus, judging by the lettering.

"No, Sergei."

"Okay. I come back later."

Nick couldn't help smiling. He turned away, but the key burned against his chest. He turned back and saw a frightening man in the crystal ball. His eyes were like Nick's, but they had no reason behind them, just pure insanity. They stared so intensely that Nick shivered, overcome by a sudden chill.

Nick walked closer to his ball, afraid to lean too close. It was the man from the tree—the charred part. It was Rasputin.

"*Privet,* Nicholai Rostov."

Nick had learned that what sounded like "privet" meant "hello." It was actually Привет—and he was so sick of learning Russian that it made his head hurt.

"Privet," Nick said, fear tingling through him like electricity. Nick wished he had an off switch. He just wanted to turn off the crystal ball entirely. He didn't want to be a Gazer. He had thought he did when it might tell him the future and make him rich. But not this. Not Rasputin. Nick shut his eyes, thinking that might make the face inside his crystal ball go away. But his mind flashed on him anyway—those insane eyes filling up his mind like a bad dream. It would be no use to run away. Rasputin would come to him in his head.

Nick opened his eyes again. "What do you want?"

"I think you know. I believe you have something I want, Nicholai."

The key burned. But Nick tried to hide the fact. "Like what?"

"Follow the trail of the Eternal Hourglass."

Nick looked in the ball. Rasputin had the hourglass in his hands. It gleamed.

"But you have it. I can see it."

"Yes. But it has lost its magical ability. It no longer works."

"How is that my fault? Why would I know anything about it?"

"Follow the trail. Follow the trail, and I'll make you a deal."

Nick eyed him warily. "What kind of deal?"

"Bring me what I seek, and I will make you far more powerful than Damian. You can leave these people and live your own life, away from all their rules, and their strange customs. What do you even know about them anyway? You can't trust them."

"But you're the bad guy. You're the one from that side of the Tree. You sent the Shadowkeepers here to drown me."

"Did I? Seems like their polar bears are the ones that tried to do that."

Nick swallowed hard.

"Gaze," Rasputin said. "Follow the trail. Betrayal is near you, Nicholai. I tell you this for your own good. Bring me what I need." He stared at Nick, who couldn't stop looking into Rasputin's eyes. They were eerie, magnetic.

And then, in a flash, Rasputin was gone.

The ball was cold.

And Nick felt utterly alone.

WHO SNEAKS INTO A LIBRARY DURING THE SUMMER?

*L*ATER THAT NIGHT, WITH DOUBLY SORE LEGS FROM horseback riding and ribs from nearly drowning, Nick woke up in the middle of the night. The key wasn't just hot; it was as if it had a heartbeat. It was throbbing.

He looked at the lettering covering both sides.

Течение реки и времени не остановить.

It had to be Russian. Theo called the Russian alphabet Cyrillic. A completely different alphabet. As if Nick didn't have enough to worry about with the new show, with having to ride the horse, with performing magic—in front of an audience under bright lights—he was learning to speak a new language. Sometimes, his brain hurt—the way it did in math class this year.

He had to know what the lettering meant. Maybe it would

reveal to him what Rasputin wanted. What the Shadowkeepers wanted badly enough to try to kill him.

He climbed out of bed and crept to his door. He opened it slightly and saw Sascha, nursing a bandaged paw from her encounter with the Shawdowkeeper, lying across his doorway.

The big tiger lifted her head, yawned, and stared expectantly at him.

"I'm going to Isabella's room," Nick whispered at the giant cat. Sascha yawned again, stretched, and padded down the hallway with him to Isabella's room. Nick knocked softly on the door, looking down one end of the hallway, then the other way, in case anyone spotted him.

A very sleepy Isabella opened the door in a long, flannel nightgown with a tiger print on it, yawning, her long hair a tangled mess of bedhead knots.

"What are you doing here?" she asked as Sascha leaned against her and rubbed her head against Isabella's hand, looking for a hug or a pat.

Now that he was there, ready to tell her about his mother's key, Nick had second thoughts. It wasn't that he thought he couldn't trust her, but he kept remembering the creature from the pool. Maybe it would be better if no one knew about the key. And then there was Rasputin's deal. And his words. Betrayal was near. Who? Isabella? Damian? Theo? Boris? Someone in the family might be the enemy.

The key throbbed urgently.

There was no getting around it. Nick needed Isabella's help.

Isabella yawned again. "Come on, Nick. Out with it."

Nick moved his T-shirt to show her the burn.

"What's that from?" she asked, squinting.

"This." He lifted up the key on the chain.

"Where'd you get it?" She touched the key. "It looks like real gold." She put it in her palm. "It's heavy, too."

"It was my mother's. I need to know what the lettering says."

The hallway was dark. "I can't really see it."

"It's Cyrillic."

"Ugh," she moaned. "I might need help. Let's ask my sister."

By now, Nick knew that Irina was Isabella's much-older sister. Isabella's father had died, and her mother no longer performed but helped care for the Grand Duchess.

"No!"

"Theo? He'll know."

Nick shook his head. "I just think it would be better for right now if we kept this a secret. I need you to get me into Damian's library. We'll look it up ourselves."

Isabella put one hand on her hip. "If we get caught, we're going to be in so much trouble."

"More trouble than a Shadowkeeper nearly killing us? Than nearly drowning? Come on, Isabella." He paused. He hated asking anyone for anything. "Please?"

"All right. Hold on." She shut her door, was gone for maybe a minute, and returned still in her old-fashioned, flannel nightgown, carrying a flashlight. "Let's go. Follow me exactly."

Isabella slid against the wall. When she came to a security camera, she said to Nick, "Get down."

The two of them got down on all fours, hidden by Sascha's immense body, and then crawled with Sascha, hoping to fool the security team into thinking that it was just the tiger on the prowl.

When they got past the camera, they slithered over to the elevator, took it one floor down, and exited. The hallway was completely dark except for a couple of dimly lit sconces on the wall. The sconces moved with them, lighting their way magically, but Isabella hissed, "Get away! Stop following us!" The sconces' flames rose higher—angry flames—but then dimmed as the sconces danced along ahead of them and farther away. Now hiding in the shadows, they entered into Damian's library, along with Sascha.

Once inside with the door shut, Isabella turned on her flashlight and pointed the beam up at the tall rows of built-in bookcases. Then she aimed her light at Nick's necklace. "Let me see it again."

He held it up and she looked at the lettering. "All right, come over here. Sascha, guard the door."

She led Nick to a book that was nearly as tall as they were, as thick as three dictionaries, and covered in a light film of dust. She pulled it out and set it on a table.

"This book contains most of the spells we use. Alphabetized. Let me see the lettering again."

Течение реки и времени не остановить.

"I wish I paid more attention in class." She bit her lip. "All right, I think this means...*Techenie reki i vremeni ne ostanovit.*" She slowly turned the thick, stiff pages. "Spells' meanings change depending on their origin—the Russian language has evolved over time."

Isabella searched, running her fingers along the pages. Nick could have sworn he heard both their hearts beating in the silent library.

"Hurry, Isabella."

"I'm trying."

She gently turned the pages, which crackled with age. After what seemed like forever in the silence of the room, she smiled in the pale beam of her flashlight. "Here it is."

Nick peered over her shoulder, but the words were all Russian and Cyrillic. "What does it mean?"

"Well, as near as I can figure, it means something like... 'Time stands still for no man.'"

"What kind of spell is that?"

She shook her head. "I don't know. I think—and I know this sounds a little crazy—but maybe…"

"What?"

"I think your mother was trying to stop time."

Nick shook his head. "I don't understand." But before he could ask Isabella any more questions, Sascha growled.

"Quiet!" Isabella whispered. She slammed the book closed and turned off her flashlight, and the three of them—Isabella, Nick, and Sascha—were plunged into pitch blackness.

AN UNLIKELY MEETING

*I*N THE DARK, AN ABSOLUTE BLACKNESS SO THICK AND oppressive that Nick couldn't even see Isabella only inches away from him, Isabella grabbed his hand and led him to a huge desk that they hid behind, crouching near the floor. Someone entered the library.

In the darkness, Sascha leaned against them, her breathing steady, her fur making Nick feel hot.

Whoever it was also had a flashlight. Nick could see its beam arching along the ceiling. The library spy moved toward several books, and they could hear him—or her—opening heavy volumes, turning pages.

Nick swallowed—although he was even afraid whoever it was could *hear* him swallow. He kept as still as possible, but every muscle ached.

The minutes seemed to pass slowly, his muscles now trembling from crouching so long. Finally, they heard the library spy emit a guttural growl of displeasure.

"Fools!" uttered the library spy.

Nick recognized the voice.

Boris.

Nick watched as the flashlight moved away from them until it was a speck. The library door opened, and then shut again.

"*That* was way too close," Isabella whispered.

They emerged from their hiding place and returned to the book of spells. It was opened to the same page that Isabella had found earlier.

"Someone knows about this spell, Nick. They went right to it."

"That was Boris."

"Are you sure?"

"I know his voice. It's the voice that tortures me in sword fighting class. I knew I couldn't trust him." He didn't tell her that Rasputin had warned him betrayal was near. "He followed us. Or he knows about the key."

Isabella bit her lip. "Boris scares me a little. He claims to control the swords used in the act, but I'm always a tiny bit afraid of him, I don't know, slipping one day and then a sword chops off Damian's head or something."

"Well, why was he in the library? In the exact same book? Looking up the exact same spell?"

"We have to find out what that key opens."

"But I have no idea what it opens. A door? A secret room? A treasure chest?"

"I've never seen a key like it before."

The two of them started toward the door when Nick spotted a glowing orb on one of the shelves.

"Look!"

"Of course!" Isabella said excitedly. "You're a Gazer. You can look into Damian's crystal balls. Come on."

Nick counted fifteen different crystal balls sitting on the shelf. Fourteen sat dark and cold. But one—about the size of a small melon—glowed with a faint bluish hue.

"I don't know what to do," Nick whispered to Isabella. "It's not my ball."

"Well, do what you do with your ball."

Nick touched the crystal. It was warm and growing hotter against his palm. He shut his eyes for a minute, and then he saw a flash in his mind.

He opened his eyes, and there inside the ball were people who looked as real as he and Isabella.

✮　✮　✮

Paris, 1900

"Monsieur Verne?"

The bearded old man turned. "Monsieur Houdini!" He crossed the room, walking with a limp, and vigorously shook the famed illusionist's hand.

"It's a pleasure to meet you."

"The pleasure is mine. Sit, sit." He gestured to a leather chair in his study.

"I am a great admirer of your work, Monsieur Verne."

"And I yours. I hear no locks can hold you."

"They have yet to make one that can, indeed."

"Cognac?"

"No, thank you. I am anxious. I must ask…these books, these novels you write that tell of a future, this book *From the Earth to the Moon* in which you write that someday man will actually travel to the moon, can they really be true?"

Verne nodded. "True. All true. Of course," he lowered his voice, "I change certain details. I don't need to arouse suspicion. But yes, someday man will travel to the moon."

"I cannot imagine. As a child, my mother told me it was made of Swiss cheese."

The two men chuckled.

"No, not Swiss cheese. But rock."

"In a flying cannon, you say?" Houdini leaned forward, trembling with excitement.

"Indeed. A rocket, actually, but for my purposes, I called it a cannon. But yes. And I named my cannon in the novel the *Columbiad*. But it will be called the *Columbia* in the future. Not much of a name change. Perhaps," he chortled softly, "I am not such a genius of the novel as people believe of me. I guess the details are so wonderful that I want to leave them all as I saw them."

"That is the amazing part. You saw it. All of your predictions? In a glass ball?"

Verne nodded. "Many years ago, in 1862, I was playing a bit of cards—gambling—with three men from Russia. One of them, a man by the name of Petrov, owed me an outlandish sum of money by the end of the night. In exchange for canceling his debt, he showed me a glimpse of the future."

"Then how did you come to possess the hourglass?"

"You know I walk with a limp."

Houdini nodded.

"You have no doubt heard the story?"

"Yes. Your nephew shot you. Was he not put into an asylum for the mentally deranged?"

"Indeed. Tragic. No one knows why a man turns to paranoia. What goes on inside the brain. And although Gaston had shot me, I found myself deeply troubled by his predicament. So I paid him a visit, under cover of night. Not even my closest friend knew. No one. I even had my carriage drop me off a half-mile from the asylum, and I walked the rest of the way, despite the great pain."

"And?"

"I saw Gaston. But he was lost in a world of insanity. I got no answers as to his state of mind when he pulled the trigger. However, as I was leaving, another inmate reached out a hand from behind a locked cell. The guard told me not to draw near, but...I sensed perhaps that this person desperately needed human touch. So I approached, warily, mind you."

"And?" By now, Houdini was almost entirely out of his seat with anticipation.

"He spoke with a Russian accent, and he thrust a piece of paper into my hand. I didn't let the guard see."

"What did it say?"

"It was the very same Russian, the one who had shown me the crystal ball. He had been imprisoned there when, drunkenly, he spoke of the future like a madman. The note begged me. If I helped secure his release, by speaking with the head of the asylum, and with, of course, my standing—I was knighted, after all—he would, in return, offer me an hourglass that stopped time."

"The rumored hourglass that belonged to Houdin?"

"Yes."

"But was it possible to secure his release?"

Jules Verne nodded and stroked his beard. "It was

secretive, of course. But yes, I vouched for him. I promised the director that as soon as the gentleman's release was secured, I would pay for his passage back to Mother Russia. He would no longer be France's problem. So again, under cover of night, the man was released. I took him by carriage to the train and arranged a series of passages for him, and in return, he gave me the hourglass. I had no reason to doubt what the hourglass can do, Monsieur Houdini. I have seen buildings as tall as the sky, and rocket ships, computers that allow people to communicate with the push of a button. And the hourglass does just as he said it would—though he did warn not to abuse it, as it can turn against a soul that does not respect its power."

"But where has it been all this time?"

"It was stolen from Houdin. Apparently, these Russians are robber barons of a type. They have no problem lying and cheating and stealing, and even gambling. A trade had been enacted—a pocket watch that was capable of stopping time, briefly, for the merest of seconds—for the hourglass. But then, the Russians discovered the magic of the pocket watch wasn't as strong. So they stole *back* the hourglass. And then, it appears to have lived a rather secretive but storied life all over Europe. Lost in a gambling match at one point. Stolen by some rather nefarious rival magicians another time. And now...now, my dear Houdini, it is here. Come."

Jules Verne stood, wincing with pain he still felt from when his crazed nephew shot him in the leg. Limping and dragging his leg slightly, he made his way to a table on which sat an object hidden beneath a velvet blanket.

Houdini stood next to him. He looked as if he could barely stop himself from ripping off the black velvet covering.

Jules Verne said, "Monsieur Houdini, may I present to you the Eternal Hourglass."

And with a flourish, he removed the velvet drape, revealing an hourglass with gold-flecked sand. Around its rim on the top and on the bottom were etched words.

In Cyrillic.

Течение реки и времени не остановить.

"What does the lettering mean?" Houdini asked, peering closely.

"According to the Russian, it is an ancient spell. *Time stands still for no man.*"

SOMETIMES ALL YOU NEED
IS A LITTLE PUSH

*T*HE NEXT MORNING AT BREAKFAST, NICK TRIED NOT TO look at Isabella. He didn't want anyone to suspect what they had done. The night before, after seeing Jules Verne in the crystal ball, they left Damian's study exactly as they found it and sneaked back to their rooms. All night long, Nick had trouble sleeping, trying to imagine what the key opened. Had his mother stolen the Eternal Hourglass and hidden it somewhere? He certainly wouldn't be surprised—seemed like he was from a long line of thieves. But then, how did Rasputin have it? And why didn't it work anymore?

All during breakfast, he concentrated on his food. He was learning to choose his foods at each meal wisely. For breakfast, one silver tureen offered *kasha*, which was sort of like oatmeal. If he added about ten teaspoons of sugar, he could almost stand it. Sometimes, he put syrup on it. Or some fruit. But always sugar—and lots of it. Same with his black tea. There were also *blinis*. But he never took the ones with fish eggs. No matter how much everyone in the family raved about caviar, he was never, ever, *ever* going to like fish eggs in jelly. So he took his *blinis* with sour cream and covered them with more sugar. In fact, he tried to cover everything with sugar. There were *ponchiki*. They were actually pretty delicious—hot donuts. But they didn't have them every day. What they *did* have every day was *borsch* and *piroshki*. *Borsch* was beet soup. Nick thought it was ten thousand shades of wrong to make soup out of beets. Chicken noodle, maybe. But beets? He had learned to eat the *piroshki,* dumplings, when they had potatoes in them. But not when they were filled with meat—or worse, prunes.

So he focused on his sugar-loaded Russian oatmeal, and drank his sugar-loaded Russian tea, and he didn't look at Isabella.

Theo entered the dining room at his usual time to collect them for school. As they walked down the hall, Nick felt himself relax. They had gotten away with it.

When they got to the classroom, Theo already had a crystal ball set up on his desk on a tall pedestal.

Already playing in the ball was a dark scene, the picture so dark, in fact, that Nick couldn't tell what was happening.

When Nick got closer, he saw it was him—and Isabella—the previous night.

"Care to explain yourselves?" Theo asked, sitting down at his desk and folding his hands.

Nick looked at Isabella. She looked back at him.

Neither of them said anything.

Theo waited.

Nick thought he could hear his own heartbeat. The cuckoo emerged from its clock.

"Tell him! Tell him!" the bird squawked.

"I'm waiting, " Theo said. "Patiently—for the moment."

Still, Nick said nothing.

"If Damian finds out you were in his library, you two will be in so much trouble you'll wish you were hedgehogs in a cage. Out with it. I can find out through magic, or you can tell me. I think it would be better to tell me. Don't you?"

Nick looked at Isabella as if to say, *We have no choice.* Suddenly, the words tumbled out of Nick—the key, the burning against his chest, the Cyrillic, what they saw in the crystal ball, and the other library spy—though he left out that it was Boris for now, and he also left out Rasputin in his crystal ball. "Theo, what does this key unlock?"

"I don't know what the key unlocks."

"Can't I gaze and…I don't know, see if my mother stole the hourglass?"

Theo touched the crystal ball, which went clear again. "Kolya, you need to understand something about magic."

"What?"

"It's everything. And it's not everything."

"I don't understand."

"Well, it's like people who dream about finding a genie and getting three wishes. It's never what you expect—sometimes, wishes have unexpected consequences. So it is with magic. We can't just gaze into the ball and ask it everything we want to know. That isn't a pure heart. That isn't our destiny. We aren't like the Shadowkeepers. Magic is everything to us. But we must use our magic respectfully. We honor it. We can't gaze every time we have a question, Kolya, or we would live in our crystal balls and in books of spells instead of amongst family."

"But...this is an important question. It's really important."

"So you think."

"But it is important!" Isabella said, leaning forward at her desk. "It is, Theo! The Shadowkeepers tried to kill Nick. We saw that thing in the pool. It was life or death, Theo."

"We each think our problems are the greatest, Nick and Isabella. But if we abuse the gift, it will turn on us. We will use it more and more for problems less and less dire. This time, it's to see what your mother may have done. Then tomorrow, it might be to see if you can find your lost shoe."

"It's not like that."

Theo shook his head. "I've seen it happen."

"But can't I see my mother? Can't I find out what happened?"

"I'm afraid not. The ball would recognize your motives, Nick. You need to unravel this without it."

"But do you think it's why the Shadowkeepers are here?"

"Now that I know what's written on the key? Yes. The Eternal Hourglass is one of our most powerful relics—and it was lost. They want it."

"What about us? Don't we want it?" Nick was suspicious. "You have a vault full of magic relics. Isn't that kind of hogging the world's magic?"

"Of course we want it. But the key burns because its rightful place is with us. It's calling us. It's calling *you*, more precisely. Now, we must turn our attention to your lessons. In particular, how you will make Sascha switch places with Isabella. We have less than two weeks to go."

"I can't do it."

"But you can. My brother was right. If you switch a hedgehog, you can switch a tiger." Theo snapped his fingers and a hedgehog appeared on his desk as if to prove a point. He snapped again, and it turned into a mouse.

"Yeah. I made my hedgehog disappear. But the hedgehog was lost for a whole night until I got it to come back. I wasn't able to do it right away. What if that happens in the show? What if I can't do it and stand there like an idiot? I'll be a joke. I'll ruin the entire show!"

"Possibly."

"And okay, let's suppose I *can* switch them. What if Isabella gets—I don't know—stuck? What then?"

"That could be messy," Theo said, wincing. "Best not to let her get stuck."

"Messy!" Nick stood up. "You're putting too much pressure on me! I don't want messy."

"That's why you need to *practice*," Theo said.

Isabella looked up at him, "Please, Nick. Practice. I don't want to be…messy."

Nick shook his head. "I quit. I quit the show."

"Too late. The posters are made."

"Posters? All this because you already made up stupid posters?" Nick started to run out of the classroom, but Sascha leaped in front of him.

"Move, Sascha!"

The tiger stared up at him, raised one paw, and used it to push Nick backward. He fell against a desk and then tumbled to the floor.

He scrambled up again. "Knock it off before I…" He felt the increasingly familiar sensation in his stomach. He shut his eyes and envisioned Isabella and Sascha switching places.

When he opened his eyes again, Isabella was standing in front of him, grinning.

"I promise I won't push you," she said, laughing. "And look." She twirled around. "All in one piece and no mess."

Fine. He had done it once now. But in front of thousands of people? The thought made him queasy.

"Do it again," Theo commanded.

"I don't think I can." Nick turned around to face Theo. "It's not easy for me. Why don't you understand that? I wasn't raised with you all. I'm a stranger here. A stranger. It's not easy."

"Nothing worth doing is easy, Kolya."

"But I *can't*."

From behind him, he heard Irina's voice. "If you think you can't, then you won't."

He turned around and saw her standing in the doorway. "But I just don't know how to do it on command. Without getting mad and feeling something in my stomach."

"You can. It's your destiny. Your mother used to be able to look at the most ferocious tiger and reduce it to a kitten with one glance. She had power. You do, too."

Nick looked at Isabella. He shut his eyes, and instead of getting mad, he focused on his stomach. There was a buzzing in his gut, and he pictured it traveling up through his body to his fingertips. He opened his eyes, and Isabella was still standing there, so he looked at her—stared *into* her—and in the blink of an eye, he was smelling Sascha's fishy breath and staring into feline tiger eyes.

He didn't even see it happen.

"I did it." He ran his fingers through Sascha's fur, marveling at its thickness. He smiled at Irina. "I did it!" He felt a pride welling up inside of him, in the place where he felt the magic. A joy that spread to his smile.

"Never doubt, Kolya. Now come along."

"Where?"

"The Grand Duchess wishes to have a private audience with you."

Nick turned to look at Isabella. She shrugged and mouthed, "I don't know."

He followed Irina out of the classroom and down the hall. She led him to a room at the very far end of the floor. Then Irina faced him.

"Let me see you. Hmm…" She smoothed his hair and straightened the collar of his shirt. "That's better. You know, no one gets a private audience with her. No one."

He swallowed. "What do I say?"

"You don't say anything. You listen. Now go on." She rapped on the door.

"Come in," came the tremulous reply.

Irina opened the heavy door with a snap of her fingers,

and Nick peered inside the room. It was dimly lit, but he could make out the Grand Duchess sitting by the window.

"Go on," whispered Irina. He felt her push him, then heard the door slam, and suddenly, he was alone with the ancient woman.

AN IMPERIAL
HISTORY LESSON

"COME SIT, KOLYA," THE OLD WOMAN SAID.

Hesitantly, he crossed the thickly carpeted floor, his shoes sinking deep into it and leaving a track of his path. The room was filled with antiques, like stepping back in time somehow. On the walls hung dozens of oil paintings, and the lamps weren't electric but were instead filled with some kind of oil or gas and flickered, their light dancing on the walls.

"Sit!" she commanded.

He sat down in a burgundy velvet chair with elaborately carved legs and arms.

"Sweet?" she asked, passing a heavy crystal bowl of hard candy. Nick took one—a candy shaped like a gift, complete with a blue bow on top—and popped it in his mouth. It tasted like an explosion of fresh blueberries on his tongue.

The Grand Duchess leaned back in her high-backed velvet chair and stared out the tall window through slightly parted velvet drapes.

"I like to sit here and remember. I miss the snow. I miss how it smelled just before a snow, the sky as white as cotton. I miss my girlhood home. This is all," she waved a hand, "designed to recreate my home, but I cannot recreate my family. I cannot recapture my girlhood. I am old, Kolya. But I like to look at snow."

Nick had never seen actual snow. He'd lived in Las Vegas for as long as he could remember. On very hot days, sometimes he liked to imagine moving to a place where it snowed. He started to ask her about the snow, about her family, but he remembered Irina's advice. He said nothing. He waited.

"Everyone calls me the Grand Duchess, but I am really her Imperial Highness. A Grand Duchess. Such a big name for such a tiny baby when I was born. When I was a little girl, my father used to worry so much, such extraordinary responsibility. Now, I am the one who worries. I am the one who stares at the snow."

Her eyes were watery. "I've never told anyone. Not the whole story. Not everything."

Nick waited patiently, but she said nothing more. Finally, he asked, "Told anyone what, Grand Duchess?"

"I survived because of him. Because of a spell."

"Him?"

"The Shadowkeeper." She spat the name like a curse. "I am Anastasia, Kolya. Do you know who I am?"

He shook his head.

"I am the daughter of the last tsar of Russia. My entire family was murdered—only I survived. But how and why—that is the tale, my little one. That is the tale." She reached out a gnarled hand and put it on his. At her touch, Nick had a flash, a vision. He saw Rasputin in a freeze-framed moment, sitting with a family in crowns and jewels. It must have been Anastasia—the Grand Duchess—and her family.

"Oh, we loved him at first. He called me *Malenkaya*. Do you know what that means, Kolya?"

Again, he shook his head.

"It means 'my little imp.'" She smiled. "The way I used to laugh with my beloved sister, Maria—I really was a little imp. I fit the name. Maria and I were the Little Pair. My two older sisters were the Big Pair." She laughed softly. "Maria and I shared a room. We did our needlepoint together. Tiny little stitches, trying to imitate our mother. Intricate. I still try to do needlepoint, but my hands don't always cooperate."

Nick looked around. Now he saw that needlepoint scenes were framed and hung on the walls, or were made into pillows for the sofa.

"Maria and I loved each other so much. We did little plays, you know. Little plays to make my papa laugh. He worried so. Russia was in turmoil. And then my baby brother was born. He was very, very spoiled." She smiled and leaned her head back and shut her eyes.

Nick waited, thinking she had fallen asleep, when she opened her eyes again. "Spoiled. He was the heir. The boy. Born after four girls. He would be the next tsar. We all coddled him. But my brother was very sick. If he fell, he would bleed. Horribly. This was long before modern medicine, so there was nothing the doctors could do for him. So my parents invited the monk into the palace. Rasputin. He would pray over my little brother. My mother believed he was curing him. But I think...I think Rasputin was really casting spells, Kolya."

Nick remembered the family tree—the charred part of the tree. He tried to picture his crystal ball, to urge it to let him see inside his own mind. He flashed on the monk's eyes. He felt as though, somehow, the monk was eavesdropping at that very moment. Nick felt him, as if his reach were inescapable.

"I loved the monk. Oh, how I loved him—he made me laugh, the monk did. And he was kind and gentle. He hugged me and would come visit me and Maria in the nursery and tell us stories. And then times grew even stranger and more dangerous. My family was arrested. We were taken to one of our palaces. Like this very building, Kolya. This entire hotel and casino is a replica right down to the plates we eat our meals on. No detail has been overlooked, my child. And in that palace, we were imprisoned—the entire imperial family."

Nick stared, afraid to break her reverie. Her eyes were pale blue and when she spoke of her girlhood, they lit up, dancing. But now they clouded.

"I know a palace like this is hardly a real prison. But the strain on Papa was terrible. We didn't know from one day to the next what would happen. Angry crowds called for our deaths. So one night, the monk cast a spell of protection over me."

Nick saw him chanting over a tiny girl, saw a black ring forming around her—a spell of protection, yes, but this one was dark.

"He loved me best. But I didn't know. I didn't know what it meant. My entire family, as well as our most beloved servants, was brought into a room, and they were murdered. All of them. By soldiers." At the memory, the Grand Duchess covered her face with her hands and wept, her delicate shoulders shaking.

Nick didn't know what to do, but he was sorry she was so sad. He stood up, stepped over to her chair, and patted her back.

When she finally looked up, her cheeks were wet with tears. She opened a small velvet purse hanging from a silver chain on her wrist and extracted a delicate lace handkerchief. She dabbed at her tears and whispered, "For years, I didn't want to live. Not without my sisters, my brother, my parents. I made my escape. But it was at a terrible cost. I now realize he had woven a spell over my parents. He blinded them to the world outside the palace windows. He blinded them to his treachery. To his greed. He stole from us. Imperial eggs, where I used to hide my treasures and jewels. And it was only later, as I sought to understand these spells, and what had happened, that I found out his true nature."

"It is the monk who is looking for me, Grand Duchess, isn't it?"

She nodded. "Indeed, Kolya."

"How can he still be alive?"

"Oh, they tried to murder him."

Nick saw flashes of gunshot, and felt an acrid poison on his tongue—just a vision, but very real. "How has he survived?"

"You know the answer. Black magic. Dark magic. They tried to shoot him, poison him, drown him. But he is indestructible. His power is too great—and still he wants more."

"But I have no power. Do you know what he wants from me?"

She shook her head.

"Did you know my mother, Grand Duchess?"

"Of course. She was so beautiful, so lovely."

"Would you know why she would hide something? What she would hide?"

"No, child. But I know when she left this place and hid from the clan, it was to make sure you were safe. I remember when she was pregnant with you."

Nick shook his head. The duchess had to be mistaken. His mother would have long since left the clan before that.

"Anyway, I don't know exactly what the Shadowkeepers want. I only know they are hungry for power. And so I look at the snow and worry. Perhaps I am very much like my father, after all. I worry, Kolya. For you. For the clan that has cared for me all this time. Rasputin is very powerful. He has indulged in dark magic for a long, long time."

"But he *did* save you."

"He did. But I think only because he hoped to one day marry me and have his children, have royal blood in his bloodline. It surely wasn't out of kindness, Kolya."

"Maybe he's misunderstood."

"No, Kolya. No. You know, before you were born, your mother left the family. And when she did, she told me she would be certain that the monk never got his hands on anything that would make him more powerful. She was very

brave, Kolya. She wasn't afraid of him. I think that was…
her downfall."

"Are you still afraid of him?"

She nodded.

"Even with Damian and Theo and the family around you?"

She nodded. "I have seen him with my own eyes, Nicholai.
You must remember that I knew him. I have seen what he
can do. He let my family be murdered in cold blood, Kolya.
Be careful. And until you know what that key opens, that key
around your neck that you think is so well hidden, don't let it
go for a minute. Not for one second. Wear it close."

"I will, Grand Duchess."

"You remind me of my little brother. If he had lived. Be
careful, Kolya. I cannot bear to lose anyone I love again."

He nodded, and then didn't know whether to bow or give
her a hug. He started to bow, but she grabbed his hand, and
pulled him to her for a hug.

"Run along now, Kolya. You have to practice for the show.
I will be in the balcony applauding on opening night."

He nodded and walked to the door. He started to say
good-bye, but he could see she was already lost in the snows
of her childhood, gazing out the window and remembering
her family.

SOME QUESTIONS ARE
BETTER LEFT UNANSWERED

*T*HE NEXT DAY, BORIS TRIED TO TEACH NICK HOW TO
control fire.

"Fire is an element. From the dawn of the Egyptians, magicians have been able to control fire. You simply let fire fly from your fingertips."

Boris gestured with his hand and a huge burst of flames flew from his fingers to the opposite wall. "When you start, we simply take a ball of fire and play with it."

Boris cupped his hands together, then uncupped them, and Nick saw a blue ball of flame, the size of a baseball, actually, dancing about a half-inch from Boris's open palms.

"Try."

"I don't want to get burned."

"You won't. Now try," he insisted.

Nick tried to imagine flames. He tried to conjure from the place in his belly, from the place that controlled the sword. He opened his eyes, and above his hand sat a tiny flame—smaller than the tongue of flame from a matchstick.

Boris laughed. "Oh, little fire from the little man. Ha!"

Nick glared sullenly at Boris.

"What?" his fighting trainer asked.

Nick was silent.

"Speak your mind, little man!" Boris's face was menacing.

"Fine," Nick snapped. "How did you get that scar?"

Boris's face turned a florid shade of red. "Why? Why is my scar important?"

Nick wanted to say, *Because I don't know if you're one of the good guys.* But instead, he said, "Because how good can you be as a fighting trainer, if you were scarred in a fight yourself?"

It was the wrong thing to say. As soon as the words left Nick's mouth, he regretted them.

Boris growled, turned from Nick, and shot flames to the ceiling. He waved his arms, and swords battled in midair, sending sparks flying and adding to the flames. He sent the swords back to the walls and made a circular motion with his arms, sending the fire into a vortex, like a tornado cloud, swirling, heat making Nick's cheeks feel like they were being burned. It hurt to breathe, the air was so hot in the room.

"Stop!" Nick screamed. "Stop it!"

"What kind of trainer am I?" Boris snorted. "Ha!" He waved his arms and the fire tornado lifted off the ground and to the ceiling, fanning out until the ceiling was in flames, then creeping down the walls, though the swords remained unharmed. The fire grew, sweeping along the floor, until only Boris and Nick stood in a circle of safety, the flames not advancing, respecting whatever circle of protection Boris had designed.

"I'm sorry!" Nick screamed.

At that, Boris lowered his arms and spoke some words to the flames, and they all disappeared. The room was back to normal, no hotter than it had been minutes before. The walls were fine, the floor not even scorched.

"I'm sorry," Nick said quietly.

"I got the scar from the Shadowkeepers. I was defending someone."

"Who?"

"That's none of your concern. But there were ten of them, and only me to defend her. I won, but I lost my eye in the process."

Boris slowly lifted his eye patch. Nick didn't want to react, but he couldn't help it as he shrunk back. Where Boris's eye should have been was just a starfish-shaped scar.

"I'm sorry."

"It was worth it to defend her."

Nick had a flash in his mind of his mother. But it was just a loose picture of her for a second, like a photograph drifting to the ground. He couldn't place it in any context.

"What are the Shadowkeepers? I mean what are they really?"

As soon as he asked the question, he felt like he had been punched in his chest as hard as someone could. Nick fell to the ground, sputtering, and thought he could vomit. He shut his eyes, but a vision came to him.

Boris knelt by his side and patted his back. "It is best not to speak of them." He turned his head and spat over his shoulder three times.

But the vision kept coming. Nick struggled to breathe, air just coming in gasps. He saw people losing their human form, their faces melting into blackness, their backs sprouting leathery wings.

He smelled them. That stench, that horrible odor. It was in his nostrils, on his clothes. It was as though they were right there with him. He clawed the air, as if he were fighting them.

Finally, he shook his head and tried to think of skateboarding, of his old life. The images didn't come, but eventually the Shadowkeepers retreated.

"They were people?" Nick asked. "*People?*"

Boris nodded. "They gave up their magician status, their

170

bloodline, for false promises of power, and were enslaved by Rasputin." Again, he spat over his shoulder three times. "Enough. We speak of good things now."

Boris helped Nick to his feet, but Nick felt weak, and his head pounded at his temples. No amount of goodness would ever let him forget what he saw.

HOUDINI'S LAST TRICK

*F*OLLOW THE *E*TERNAL *H*OURGLASS.

That had been Rasputin's advice. After seeing and feeling the Shadowkeepers while training with Boris, Nick skipped dinner. He had no appetite; it was as if the Shadowkeepers lingered over him. It reminded him of times when he knew he was getting sick or coming down with something, a dragging sensation, a tiredness.

Alone in his room, he stared at his crystal ball. He didn't want to follow the path of the hourglass. But at the same time, he knew he'd never unlock the key's secret until he did.

He looked at Vladimir. "I think I have to Gaze. Sorry."

The hedgehog hurried to a corner of his gilded cage and burrowed under soft grasses, hiding his eyes.

Nick reluctantly placed his hands on the ball and searched in the clear crystal for clues to the hourglass.

✩ ✩ ✩

Detroit's Grace Hospital, October 31, 1926
Harry Houdini lay close to death, a pallor on his face, sweat coursing in rivulets at his temples. A doctor stood over him and spoke to a nurse in a starched white uniform.

"Ruptured appendix…a shame. And on Halloween. Strange indeed. We'll keep trying to bring down the fever, but this is most dangerous."

She nodded, made a note on a clipboard, and followed the doctor from the room.

Suddenly, the linoleum-tiled room filled with a black smoke, and Rasputin appeared. He leaned over Houdini's hospital bed, its railings silver and gleaming.

"You should have stuck to illusion, Mr. Houdini, and never have dabbled in real magic."

Houdini, feverish and delirious, opened his eyes. "You…" he managed to whisper.

"Yes," Rasputin smiled. "Now tell me where your wife stores the Eternal Hourglass."

Houdini mouthed the word, "Never," his breathing labored.

Rasputin touched Houdini, and the magician let out a cry of agony.

"Tell me where it is, and I will lift this spell and you will be healed. For all appearances, you have appendicitis, but pulsing through your abdomen is powerful magic—it will kill you. Slowly. Painfully. Unless you tell me what I want to know."

Houdini shook his head.

"I can always ask your beloved Bess myself. Give her a taste of real magic."

Houdini's eyes registered terror. He motioned for Rasputin to lean closer, and he whispered something in Rasputin's ear.

Rasputin stood and smiled. "Excellent."

He turned from the bed.

Houdini flung his head from side to side and moaned.

Rasputin lifted one finger. "When will mortals learn?" With a single gesture, Houdini gasped.

Rasputin disappeared.

And at 1:26 in the afternoon in room 401, Harry Houdini died.

A BARGAIN STRUCK

*T*HE NEXT DAYS PASSED IN A BLUR OF REHEARSALS UNTIL Nick was exhausted. Then the night before the opening, as he was trying to get some sleep, he heard a frantic knocking on his door.

He opened it to find Theo, Damian, and Irina at his door. "What?"

"Come with us," Damian demanded.

"What is it?"

But Damian was already down the hallway. Nick was led into the security room. There, frozen on the banks of monitors, was the most frightening man he had ever seen staring back from each screen. His beard was unkempt, and his clothes were black. But it was his eyes, his expression, that made Nick shiver. His eyes were dead. Cold in a way he couldn't imagine. The eyes of death, of evil. Of murder. It was Rasputin. The man he had seen in his crystal ball.

"He's here," Damian said. "This man!" He touched the screen. "He's here, leading the Shadowkeepers."

"He's here for me," Nick said solemnly.

"But look here." Theo pressed some buttons and the security tapes rewound. People moved backward, and then Theo found the precise spot on the tape he wanted Nick to see. "There!"

He leaned in close, and there it was in the man's hand. "The Eternal Hourglass?"

Irina nodded. "Indeed." She spoke to the head of security. "Blow up the hourglass—extra close-up."

More buttons were pressed, and there it was—the hourglass with the Cyrillic along the top.

Nick didn't tell them that he already knew Rasputin had the hourglass. He touched the key as it grew warm against him.

"He's here," Damian said. "With the hourglass. In his hands. It can only mean destruction."

"We can't have the show tomorrow night," Nick said. "We'd be crazy to have the show."

Damian stood, his face impassive. So Nick turned to Theo. "Come on. You don't think we should go on. What if he's planning on doing something? What if he tries to kill me? Or the Grand Duchess?"

Theo whispered, "It's out of my hands, Kolya. Out of my hands." He gestured as though he was washing his palms.

"You've got to be kidding me! Why do you listen to Damian? Why is he in charge? He doesn't listen to anyone. All he cares about is his face blown up two stories high on posters. He wants to be famous, and he doesn't care who gets hurt."

Irina put a hand on Nick's arm. "Hush, Nick. It's not like that."

He wrested his arm away from her. "It *is* like that. He doesn't listen. He's just an arrogant jerk! He'll end up killing us all."

With that, he pushed past Irina, Theo, and Damian and ran out into the hallway and back down to his room. He commanded the door to open, then shut the door and locked it. He didn't care what Damian wanted. He just wouldn't show up for the stupid show tomorrow. He would run away. He'd go back to the Pendragon. To Grandpa. To his dad. Forget about the whole show and this crazy family with their awful food.

He would skateboard, and he'd study harder and get a B in math this year—that had to be easier than studying Russian. He'd play video games, and he would pretend he never had a crystal ball, never saw a vision, never rode an Akhal-Teke.

But even as he thought it, he knew he couldn't. He couldn't leave this life. That man—the crazed monk, the

Shadowkeepers' leader—would find him. He'd put his dad and grandpa in danger. Rasputin could make them sick and kill them just as he had Harry Houdini.

So he would run away on his own.

That thought scared him, too. He had no money. What would he live on? How far could he get all alone?

And then he looked around the room.

His mother's things. That very first night in his room, they told him everything in here was hers; it was her room as she left it, his inheritance.

He ran to his dresser and picked up her brush and comb set. It was heavy and silver. That had to be worth something.

He looked over at the shelves. The eggs! The jewel-encrusted eggs! They glittered with emeralds and gold. They had to be worth a fortune. Heck, he could get all the way to Belize if he sold them. He could run away, and no one would ever find him.

And then he felt an icy chill pass over him, even as the key burned hotter than ever.

The Grand Duchess's words rang in his head.

He stole from us. Imperial eggs, where I used to hide my treasures and jewels.

"That's it. The eggs!"

He ran to the shelf where four eggs sat. The Grand Duchess's family had eggs made for them—rare, jeweled eggs. People hid things in them. He pulled the key from around his neck.

All four of the eggs in his room had small locks that never would have fit the key. But he knew about another egg—the biggest, grandest egg, encrusted in gold and jewels, and covered in a beautiful, cobalt blue enamel. That egg had a larger keyhole.

The one in the vault.

He would break into the vault, open the egg, and get whatever was inside. He touched the key, and it burned hotter than it ever had and throbbed against his heart, beating time with his own heartbeat. That was it. Whatever Rasputin wanted was in his mother's egg inside that vault. And he was the rightful heir to that egg, so it wasn't exactly like stealing.

Nick ran over to his ball. "Rasputin," he whispered. "Rasputin!"

He touched his ball. Nothing happened.

Pure of heart. Pure of heart.

"Look," Nick spoke to his ball. "I'm not doing this for me. I'm doing it for my family. I don't want them harmed. What he wants, my mother took from him. I know it. I need to make a deal with him."

He took several deep breaths, and the ball grew hazy.

"Hey! Nick!"

"Sergei," Nick hissed. "Get out of here. Now! Not today."

"No, listen. I found a tap-dancing llama. He's got to be seen to be believed. I'm teaching him to do the *Barynya*."

"What's that?"

"Russian folk dance. Your family will love it. He's cheap, too. Come on, Nicholai, do me a favor. Talk to Damian."

Nick gritted his teeth. "Sergei, I'm telling you—not now. Come back in a couple of days." He added, under his breath, "If I survive."

"Fine. But a llama like this won't last long."

Sergei disappeared, and the ball grew black, an oily black. Nick knew Rasputin was near.

"You summoned me?" The monk's face appeared inside the orb. "Do you have what I am seeking?"

"I'll have it tomorrow night, after the show."

"Where shall we meet?"

"Not so fast. I want to strike a deal."

"What kind of deal? I thought you were going to join me, leave these people with their rules and their superstitions like Russian peasants."

"I'll join you—on the condition you leave them alone. Forever."

The monk was silent, and then smiled. "It is a deal. Provided you have what I seek."

"Then we meet in the desert."

"I'll find you."

"Remember our bargain."

"Of course. I always honor my bargains."

The crystal ball went dark. Nick stared into its cool clarity again. He knew Rasputin was a liar, but he had no choice. He hoped he knew what he was doing.

A MOTHER'S CHOICE

N ICK SPENT ALL NIGHT FORMULATING HIS PLAN. HE didn't tell anyone, not even Isabella.

The next day, he ate breakfast with the family, feeling sick to his stomach. He was planning on facing down the Shadowkeepers. That was scary enough.

But first, he had to perform in front of thousands of people tonight. If he was being honest with himself, Nick didn't know which scared him more. He kind of thought it was performing. Then there was the teeny-tiny little matter of breaking into the vault, stealing his mother's egg, and meeting up with the monk who brought evil into the casino.

Damian ordered him to "rest" before the show. How was he supposed to do that? He went to his room and found himself pacing back and forth, back and forth. He took his skateboard out from under the bed, where he hid it, and he slid it across his bedroom floor. If everything went right, he might even be able to go back to being a normal kid. About two hours before show time, he heard a knock on his door. When he opened it, Theo stood there.

"Can I come in?"

Nick nodded.

Theo entered his room. He placed a crystal ball on the bed.

"What? I have my own ball."

"Look," Theo commanded. "This ball belongs to me. It's very powerful."

"I don't understand."

"Look…and you will."

Nick took a deep breath and stared into the ball. At first, he couldn't see anything. But then a woman came into focus. It was his mother.

And Theo and Damian were there. Damian was leaning over a baby.

"Is that me?" Nick whispered.

"Yes."

Nick exhaled in amazement and watched the scene unfold.

"I told you, I'm not coming back. Not now. Not ever." His mother crossed her arms. Her hair was beautiful and shiny and fell down to her waist. "I won't leave this place."

"Surely, cousin dearest, you cannot be happy married to a human. A mortal who is, I might add, a terrible illusionist," Damian said. He shuddered dramatically, as if trying to shake off a horrid image from his mind.

She picked up the chubby little baby and handed him a silver rattle. The baby cooed and giggled.

"I am very happy here, Damian. I love my husband."

"How is that possible?"

"Because for once, it's not about the family, the clan, the magic, the Shadowkeepers, the battle. It's about me, and my husband, and this baby. It's about my own life."

"But this baby has a *destiny*, Tatyana, that not even you can deny."

"No. I won't allow it!" She stamped her foot. "He's going to grow up far from you. From your influence. Far from the Grand Duchess. Far from the prophecy."

Theo stepped between her and Damian and knelt down in front of her. "You don't understand, my darling."

"What?"

"You cannot hide from a prophecy. It's prophetic. That means it's fulfilled, no matter what. You cannot hide a prince and stop him from being a prince. You cannot take a light, hide it under a thick velvet blanket, and stop it from being a light. You cannot take your magic and stop using it and not be a Magickeeper anymore. You are, whether you choose to use your magic or not. It would be like humans with type O blood. You can't *decide* you don't want type O blood running through your veins, because it's there nonetheless."

"No." Her lip quivered. "I won't let you near him. I want you both to leave. I want you to leave now."

Damian snapped, "Fine!"

But Theo didn't stand up.

Damian stormed to the door. "Theo! Now!"

"I'll be there in a minute."

"You're wasting your time. She's stubborn as a mule, just like when we were children. I'll meet you downstairs."

Damian opened the door, walked through, and then slammed it.

"Let me whisper a protection spell over him."

She nodded.

"*Oberezhnyj scheet predkov hranit menia. Oberezhnyj scheet predkov hranit menia. Oberezhnyj scheet predkov hranit menia.*" Theo touched the baby's forehead.

"I'm not coming back, Theo."

"We can't protect you out there alone."

"I can protect myself."

"What is that key? That key around your neck?"

She closed her blouse, buttoning the top button. "Don't concern yourself, Theo. It's my insurance policy. If they find me, I will make a trade. The key for my child being left alone."

"Don't. Don't be naïve. You cannot negotiate with them. They cannot be trusted."

"Please, Theo. Just go. You call attention to me by being here. Their spies are everywhere."

"We weren't followed. We made sure of that."

"Just go."

"I love you, Tatyana."

She sniffled. "I love you, too, Theo. You were always my favorite. The one to protect me from your bully of a brother."

"He cares about you, about the clan. He loves you. He loves us all."

She nodded. "But he loves himself most of all."

Theo stood and leaned in to kiss her cheek. He lingered a moment, stroked her chin, and then turned to leave. But first, he looked down at the child and touched the baby's soft, dark hair. "He's beautiful. He really is."

She nodded. "I'm so sorry, Theo."

He shook his head sadly. "I'm sorry, too. Good-bye," he said, and shut the door behind him.

Tatyana rocked the baby. "*Oberezhnyj scheet predkov hranit menia. Oberezhnyj scheet predkov hranit menia. Oberezhnyj scheet predkov hranit menia.*"

She brought the baby into the bedroom and put him in his simple wooden crib. At the foot of the bed sat a large trunk with a brass clasp. She opened the trunk and pulled out the Eternal Hourglass. She touched its gold rim, then shook her head and put it away, shutting the trunk.

She leaned over the baby's crib. "Oh, little Kolya, your grandfather won the Eternal Hourglass in a poker game. I told him it was trouble—it brings too much attention. But he'll never change. Always on the hunt for relics. But this one...this one is too dangerous. I'm going to destroy it to protect us all."

Suddenly, black smoke appeared from under the door, just wisps at first, but increasing until it crawled like a demon's fingers along the floor, pooling like an oil slick.

Tatyana rose and screamed the words, *"Oberezhnyj scheet predkov hranit menia!"*

The smoke swirled around her and the baby. Tatyana coughed and screamed. The baby cried in fear.

Soon, there was only blackness.

✤　✤　✤

Nick didn't want Theo to see him cry. He swallowed hard.

"I loved her, Nick. And we brought them to her doorstep. Mark my words, they would have found her, and without the spell, it would have been worse. You wouldn't have survived. I should have cast the spell over the both of you, but not even my magic was that strong."

"Why are you showing me this, Theo?"

"Whatever you are planning, whatever you are thinking, it's better to be with us than go it alone."

"What are you talking about?"

"You need to tell me what you're planning."

"I'm not planning anything," Nick snapped.

"I sense it. Your key, it's somehow changed. It's vibrating."

"So?"

"So I can only assume that means you know what it opens, young cousin. Don't make your mother's mistake."

"*She* didn't make a mistake!" Nick screamed with fury. "*You* did. *Damian* did. You said it yourself. You underestimated them. You thought no one followed you, but obviously one of them did. Go away, Theo."

"Kolya, trust me. Tell me what the key opens. Tell me, please. I am begging you."

"Go away." Nick turned his back to Theo. "I have to prepare for the show."

A ROSE OF
A DIFFERENT HUE

ICK SAT ATOP MASLOW IN THE PITCH DARKNESS. THEY were beneath a trapdoor-like contraption. In the darkness, Nick's heart beat like a drum. He could hear his blood pulsing through his own veins. Maslow occasionally twitched with anticipation or stamped a hoof.

Nick heard the orchestra begin playing. That was something else he discovered about the family. Those that didn't perform magic played the violin, the balalaika, or the piano. They were marvelous musicians, and the orchestra at the Winter Palace Casino was, according to the critics, one of the greatest in the world. What made it even more remarkable was that no outside musicians played—only family. Critics marveled that one family could have so much talent.

The orchestra's vibrations sent a ripple through him, as

if he could feel each loud chord. The music, he knew, was traditional folk, although later, they would play a piece by Damian's favorite composer, Shostakovich.

Slowly, the trapdoor parted, and he and Maslow were elevated out of the floor. Nick's hands were sweaty as he held Maslow's reins. His hair clung damply to the nape of his neck. He and the horse rose from beneath the trapdoor as the audience quieted and the orchestra stopped playing. In the silence, a spotlight illuminated them, reflecting on the glittering small gems sewn on his costume and on Maslow's gold and emerald harness. Nick's sword was in a sheath by his side. Its hilt gleamed in the light.

The orchestra began playing again, and the music rose to a crescendo echoing through his belly. Nick waited for his cue: the striking of the timpani.

At the sound, which felt like his own pulse from deep within, Nick dug his heel into Maslow's side. Maslow leaped from his spot and onto the metal pathway. The horse's hooves clipped like thunder along the path, competing with the timpani's boom-boom-boom.

"Yah!" Nick shouted, and Maslow charged faster. Nick literally felt himself rising up out of his saddle, as if he was flying himself. He was terrified but excited, his hair whipping around his face.

He could see, in a blur, the snowbank ahead of him, white, cold, and glistening. Tightening his legs around Maslow, he urged the horse to leap. They flew over the snowbank as the audience shrieked with pleasure and excitement. Next, they leaped over two growling polar bears.

Two enormous Siberian tigers rose up on their hind legs and roared. Maslow rose up on his hind legs. The animals appeared to do battle.

Nick leaped from his horse, sliding across the glacial blue ice, and appeared to stab the first tiger with his sword.

Standing astride the fallen tiger, Nick stared down at the other beast, Sascha, who roared with ferocity that echoed and reverberated to the base of Nick's spine. His scalp tingled.

Nick gestured with his hand and said a silent prayer this would work, and in an instant, the tiger fell to the floor. Nick reach a hand down to Sascha, and in the white tiger's place lay Isabella in a white gown with a fur collar.

Nick helped her stand and took a deep bow while she curtsied, each of them grinning.

The theater erupted in a cacophony the likes of which he had never heard before. It was so loud, his teeth rattled. People screamed, "Bravo!" and shouts rang from the topmost seats in the theater.

"Bow again," Isabella shouted, smiling and raising her arms high. "You did it!"

"*We* did it!" he screamed, barely able to hear himself over the roar.

They bowed deeply, then she curtsied again. People in the first three rows threw red roses, which landed at their feet. Someone threw a bouquet at Isabella, and she scooped it up, smelling the fresh lilies wrapped in cellophane tied with a giant bow.

"Damian is a genius," she shouted above the noise. "We're a huge hit."

"I know," Nick beamed. Not even pulling off a C-plus on his math final felt this good.

And then Nick spied it.

A single black rose landed at his feet.

He looked up, but the spotlights were so bright, they blinded him. The curtain fell, and he picked up the black rose and faced Isabella.

"They're here."

All the color drained from her face.

Above them, he saw a black oil stain creeping along the ceiling. A foul stench surrounded them. Around him, he saw fear crossing over the faces of his family.

There. He thought it.

His family.

"Come on, Isabella."

"Where can we go?"

The shadows grew in number.

"Do you trust me?" he asked her.

She looked him in the eyes and nodded.

"Come on, then. I know what they want."

He grabbed her hand in the chaos and led her to the underground passageway beneath the theater and then to the elevator to the vault—the one with no buttons.

"Isabella, the Shadowkeepers won't rest until I get them what they want."

"What's that?"

"I'm not sure. But I *am* sure it has to do with this key and a Fabergé egg in the family vault. I'll understand if you don't want to help me break in, but I'm going to do it."

"Are you insane? You are. My cousin has officially lost his mind."

"I haven't. Please, Isabella. Between your magic and my magic, we can do it."

She sighed. "All right, I hope you know what you're doing. Damian's going to kill us."

"If the Shadowkeepers don't kill us all first."

The elevator doors opened, and the grizzly bear was inside. It growled, and Isabella held up her hand. "Silence. Obedience."

The bear shrank back, and they hopped on the elevator, doors shutting with a whoosh. Soon, they were hurtling farther underground, to the vault.

The doors opened again, and Nick was in the area where Theo had taken him through the wall.

"I don't think I'm strong enough to create an opening like Theo did," Nick said. "We're going to have to get through the booby traps."

They raced to the door of the vault.

"You're crazy," Isabella said. "Damian designed the booby traps himself. Only he can get past them."

"No. We just have to think like him."

"Let's go get him," Isabella said. "He'll help us. He will. If what you say is true, then he will help us."

"No. This is the only way."

She sighed and finally nodded.

"Okay, first this lock." Nick stared at it. It was a combination lock like on his locker at school, but there were letters instead of numbers, and the letters were in Cyrillic. "If you were Damian," Nick asked Isabella, "what would you use as the code?"

They stared at the lock, and then she smiled. "Anastasia." She twisted the lock to the various letters of the Grand Duchess's given name. "He is devoted to her."

"I didn't think he was devoted to anyone."

"No," she shook her head. "He has tea with her once a day." She spun the lock until they heard a click.

"We're in."

The door swung wide. Instantly, two white tigers, each larger than Sascha, bounded toward them. Isabella spoke to them in Russian, but they still came at them.

The tigers snarled and snapped. Their teeth gleamed. They snarled so close that their saliva dripped to the floor near Nick's shoes, forming a small puddle.

Isabella repeated her commands.

"Why aren't they stopping?"

"I don't know." She hesitated and then said, "Wait!" She spoke a new command, and this time they retreated.

"What happened?"

"The Russian language changes through history. Damian wouldn't use modern Russian. If he cast the spell, he would make it trickier and use commands from the Grand Duchess's time."

"Good thing you've been passing all Theo's language exams."

"It's because I don't make my bed on exam day."

"No, it's because you are way smarter than I am at language."

They passed through the room, the tigers now purring like kittens.

At the far end of the room was another door. It had an ordinary handle. Nick tried it, and the door opened, revealing yet another room with a dark marble floor.

Isabella started to run through the door when Nick grabbed her.

"Wait!"

"What?"

"This isn't right. With Damian, if there's an easy way or a hard way, he'll always choose the hard way. Irina said so herself. This was too easy. Way too easy."

He looked down at his performance costume and ripped off a button. He tossed it onto the floor. Instead of landing *on* the floor, it fell *through* the floor, and it was a full two or three seconds before they heard the faint *ping* of it landing somewhere below.

"Oh, he's good," Isabella said.

"It's too far to jump across." Nick stared at the far end of the next room. "So now what?"

"How good are your levitation skills?"

"Weak. I'm so new at it."

"Well, that's our only shot."

Nick swallowed hard.

Levitation was a leap of faith. A leap of clarity, Theo told him. Nick had done it all of three times, and never for more than a few seconds.

Nick centered himself, took a deep breath, grabbed Isabella's hand, and stepped forward. A leap of belief.

The two of them hovered. Nick had the sensation of walking on wind. They floated over the marble floor, and when Nick looked down, he could see the floor shifting aside and the chasm beneath them.

"Don't look down," Isabella told him. "Concentrate."

They reached the next door, which also turned easily. Another empty room. Nick peered down. The floor looked solid.

The two of them stepped down on the floor. As soon as they did, Nick noticed the walls. They were covered with spiders. Big, fat, hairy spiders.

"Let's just run."

"Nick?"

"Yeah?"

"Look up."

Above them was a mama spider about six feet in diameter.

"I feel like a fly," he whispered.

"What do we do?"

Nick thought of Boris's fire skills. He conjured a fireball in his hands, but it was small.

"I hope you've got something bigger than that. Please tell me you do."

The mama spider shot a web at them. Nick tossed the fireball at her. She retreated, squealing. But now her baby spiders—which were all the size of Nick's fist—started toward them. Nick said to Isabella, "Cast a spell of protection around us. A circle. I'll do the fire."

She spoke, while he concentrated on the fire. Soon, fire swirled all around them, small at first, but growing. He created a tornado of blue and purple and orange flames while they stood in the center, safe.

Nick inched along, smelling charred spider flesh, a stench remarkably like the one produced by Mystery-Meat Mondays at school. When they reached the door, he tried the handle. It turned.

Nick opened the door. They were in the vault.

CHAPTER
23

THE KEY
AND THE EGG

ISABELLA STARED IN AWE AT THE RELICS.

"Do you have any idea how powerful all this stuff is?"

"Yeah. I have some idea."

"Nick, do you really think you can negotiate with them?"

"I think it's my only chance. Our only chance."

He stood in front of the glass case that held his mother's egg. He concentrated on it, touched the glass, and found that his hand could slip through the glass and touch the egg.

As soon as his fingers touched it, he saw Boris. In his vision, Boris protected his mother *and* the egg. It was just a flash, but Boris was somehow tied to the egg.

Nick pulled the egg out of the case. The vibrations of the key made a high-pitched sound. Nick took the shaking key and put it in the lock on the center of the egg.

Nick heard a click. Then the egg started playing a song, the notes sounding like those of a harp.

He turned the lock and lifted the top of the egg.

Inside, the egg was mirrored. There was a blue velvet cushion in the center of it, and nestled on the cushion was a blue velvet pouch embroidered with the family crest.

"Look, Nick," Isabella whispered.

Heart pounding against his chest, Nick lifted the pouch. He opened it, peering inside, expecting diamonds or rubies or family jewels.

Instead, it was sand. Gold-flecked sand, to be sure. But still...*sand?*

Nick furrowed his brow. He tried to think of what his mother had done, what her secret was, and why the Shadowkeepers had come all this way for what amounted to sand. He remembered the words on the key.

Techenie reki i vremeni ne ostanovit.

Time stands still for no one.

Time stands still for no one.

Time stands still for no one.

He repeated the words over and over again.

The Eternal Hourglass stopped time. Harry Houdini would have wanted it so he could stop time and escape his shackles.

But a Shadowkeeper could do anything with stopped time. He could kill someone while the person was frozen, or steal, or deceive. But the Shadowkeepers already *had* the hourglass with its golden sand.

Unless.

Nick looked at the sand. He moved over to a beam of light illuminating the case and peered into the velvet pouch under the bright light. The sand glinted and glistened. It gave off a heat like the key. It was magic sand.

What if his mother stole some sand from the Eternal Hourglass? What if the hourglass didn't work anymore?

Rasputin didn't want the hourglass—he already had it.

He didn't want Nick's key.

He didn't want an imperial egg or jewels.

He wanted the stolen sand.

Without it, the hourglass didn't work, and Rasputin and the Shadowkeepers couldn't stop time. Without it, the relic was incomplete.

"AWESOME"

EAVING THE VAULT WAS A LOT EASIER THAN GETTING INSIDE
it. Nick and Isabella simply ran. They reached the
elevator and took it to the lobby, then raced through it
and out the front doors, tourists staring at them in their
costumes.

"Nick!" Isabella stopped at the sidewalk. "I've never left
the hotel before."

"You won't melt. Come on!"

"I can't!"

"You can, Isabella. The world is an okay place. This is the
only way. Come on. We have to meet him, trade the sand for
leaving us alone."

She looked at him, fear in her eyes. "I can't, Nick."

"You said you trusted me. I need you to keep trusting me."

Finally, she nodded, and the two of them dashed down the gleaming Las Vegas Strip.

Eventually, Nick turned a corner. And just as he had planned, Maslow was waiting.

"Good horse!" he beamed.

Nick helped Isabella onto Maslow's back and then slipped his foot in the stirrup, climbed on in front of her, and settled into the saddle.

"Let's see if this horse can really ride in the desert."

"What are you doing?" Isabella screamed as the horse clipped down the sidewalk.

"Escaping. Just hold on!"

Isabella tightened her arms around his middle as Maslow leaped over a BMW, then a limousine. From down the street a bit, Nick heard police sirens.

"What if the police follow us?"

Nick looked back. "Once we hit the desert sands, police cars will be no match for Maslow."

Isabella craned her neck. "I know I should be scared, but this is awesome!"

Nick thought of how she had grown up in the confines of the family casino. Around them were roller coasters and lights and people and billboards and the staccato animation of signage announcing every performer in Vegas.

Nick urged Maslow to go faster. Behind them, in the far

distance, he could hear the hissing sounds of Shadowkeepers. From far above them came the flapping of their wings.

The horse was tireless. Eventually, Nick reached a point where he could turn off the crowded street and into the desert. He pulled on the reins, but the horse needed no direction. It was as if the Akhal-Teke instinctively knew where to go.

In the desert, stars stretched across the sky. A full moon rose high above them, and across the moon, high up like clouds of death, flew the leathery Shadowkeepers.

FIRE, WATER, WIND, AND SAND

NICK KNEW MASLOW COULD TRAVEL OVER TWO HUNDRED miles in the desert without water. He was counting on the horse's endurance. He was counting on the legend of the Akhal-Teke's extraordinary breed.

Maslow seemed to revel in his freedom and the challenge of trying to outrun the Shadowkeepers. The horse galloped with wild abandon, not even seeming to break a sweat. Instead, he gained speed the farther they rode into the desert.

Nick felt the cool, sandy wind in his face, and had he not been trying to outrun Shadowkeepers, he would have been excited by his night ride. The desert was chilly at night, and goose bumps rose on his arms. Isabella shivered in her short-sleeved gown. But he didn't know whether that was from fear or from the chill. Or both.

He drove the horse farther into the desert, but always, the Shadowkeepers flew like wraiths overhead, hissing and screeching with inhuman cries.

Isabella asked him, "Do you know what you're doing? Please tell me you know what you're doing."

He nodded. "I do."

"You can't hope to face them alone. You're not powerful enough yet. You need Damian. And Theo."

At the thought of Damian and Theo, Nick felt a spark of anger in his gut.

"I don't need them. I figured out what they wanted. I figured out what the key opened. It was me who broke into the vault."

"You sound like a Shadowkeeper, impressed with your own power."

"I know what I'm doing. These beasts thrive on the night. We're running until the sun comes up."

On they rode. Maslow was tireless, and Nick hoped whatever spell Irina cast on the horse gave him extra stamina for good measure. The two of them seemed as one, and he reveled in the fact that he only had to think of a direction for the horse to shift.

Nick was exhausted, though. By the time the first rays of dawn stretched like gray fingers across the sky, he felt blistered and bruised, and he was certain Isabella felt the same.

The two of them were flecked with sand and grit. It clung to their cheeks, and made their eyes itch with each blink. It coated their hair and mouths.

But as the sun rose, one by one, the flying Shadowkeepers fell away, shrieking and hissing and arcing high, like hawks, before disappearing. Finally, none were overhead.

Nick slowed Maslow to a trot and then to a walk.

"We did it, Isabella." He couldn't believe it. His plan had worked!

"Let me down. Let me off this horse for just a bit," she begged. He knew how she felt. If he never climbed in another saddle again, it would be too soon.

The two of them dismounted. Nick's legs trembled, his muscles barely working. His legs cramped in his calves and his hamstrings. He fell to his knees, and Isabella lay down on the sand, so exhausted he thought she would fall asleep right there. Nick scooped up a handful of sand and put it in his pocket. The sun rose in the desert sky, painting it with rose and violet hues, not a cloud visible.

Maslow's sides heaved. The horse walked over to a scrubby plant and nibbled at desert grass. He whinnied softly.

And then they saw him. Coming over a rise in the sand.

The monk.

Isabella scrambled up and stood next to Nick. "I wish Sascha was here."

Nick swallowed but found his mouth was parched, no saliva to wet his tongue or lips.

"Hello, little Kolya, so we meet again." The monk was dressed in clothes from his time with the tsar's family: long black robes. But he didn't even sweat in the rising, early morning heat.

"Don't call me that. You don't get to call me that."

"I haven't seen you since you were a little baby in your mother's arms. You cried then. She cried as she begged for my mercy. I will make you cry again."

The monk's eyes were crazed, an eerie pale color, and his unkempt beard fell past his waist. His beard was so scrubby and dirty, Nick thought it looked as though wild mice had scampered through it.

"What do you want?" Isabella demanded.

"Ask your cousin there. He knows. Or has he hidden his secrets from his family, like his mother did before him?"

Isabella looked over at Nick questioningly.

Nick pulled his mother's hidden pouch from his pocket. "He wants this. It's no secret. Do we have a deal?"

"Of course. You join me, you give me the missing sand, and I will leave your family alone. You don't join me…and you will suffer. They all will suffer."

"Nick?" Isabella's voice sounded panicked.

Nick answered, "He's had the Eternal Hourglass all along. It just doesn't work. And he hasn't known why. This is what he wants. My mother stole sand from the hourglass. Without it, the hourglass can't stop time."

"But if you make this trade, Nick, he'll be too powerful. You haven't thought this all the way through."

"It doesn't matter now. *Mamasha tvoya-to umerla ni za chto ni pro chto*," said the monk. He spat at the ground.

"What does that mean?" Nick demanded. "What did he say?"

Isabella grabbed his hand, squeezed, and whispered, "Your mother died in vain. It was him, Nick. He was *there*."

"Give me the sand, Kolya," the monk said, malevolence in his voice, "and I might let you live."

"Leave now, Rasputin, and I might not kill you," said someone behind Nick and Isabella—Damian's voice.

Nick looked over his shoulder and saw Damian, Irina, and Theo, standing shoulder to shoulder. He felt a surge of courage, and loosened the tassel of the velvet pouch. "Come near me or *my family*, and I will dump this sand into the desert. The hourglass will be ruined for eternity."

"You wouldn't dare."

Nick loosened the tassel more and opened the pouch. "I would. Without hesitation."

The monk stared at Isabella. Without his even moving a finger, using only his stare, she suddenly gasped and fell to the desert floor, pale, unconscious.

Irina raced to her side. "Isabella!" she shrieked as Damian levitated and flew toward the monk.

"You will regret that!" Damian shouted.

With a flash, a lightning bolt struck the desert sand near the monk, leaving a deep imprint and a valley of smoldering blackness and stench.

The monk struck back, sending the black, deadly oil of the Shadowkeepers, oozing like an oil rig gone awry, toward Isabella and Irina.

"The sand will be lost forever!" Nick said, raising his arm with the velvet pouch in his hand. With a vicious strike of pain, the pouch fell from his hand and started traveling, as if it moved of its own volition, across the sand toward the monk.

Nick bit his lip to keep from screaming out in pain and dove for the pouch, sand flying into his eyes and nearly blinding him. Damian, meanwhile, spoke words of a spell that sent a flush of water, like a sudden swirling flash flood in a rainstorm, to sweep away the black oil from Irina and Isabella.

Nick reached the pouch, and though it now burned to his touch, he grabbed it and clutched it to his chest. He spoke his mother's spell.

"*Oberezhnyj scheet predkov hranit menia.*"

"Your family can't protect you, anymore than they could protect Anastasia. Only I have that power." Rasputin turned his hate-filled gaze upon Damian, and Nick watched, aghast, as his powerful cousin screamed out in pain, clutched his heart, and fell to the desert floor.

Nick undid the pouch completely and poured sand into his hand. "I will do it!"

"You foolish child. Don't you realize they will do whatever they can to get the hourglass? You are throwing your league in with them, but they want the relic just as much as I do. They would kill you for the relic, just as I will. This is an age-old battle for relics, and you're just caught in the middle."

Nick shook his head. "No. They want the relic to *honor* magic. To do good with it."

"Is that why they have stolen the relics through time? They are nothing more than thieves. They store them in their vault. They hoard them."

"Go ahead, Kolya," Theo said. He stood behind his younger cousin. "He's wrong. It's the family. It's all we have ever cared about. Protecting each other. Loving each other. Throw the sand away. It's the love we have that matters."

"Like you loved Tatyana?" the monk asked. "You led me to her like the pebbles Hansel and Gretel left in the woods."

Nick felt Theo's hand on his shoulder. "I may have led you to her, but it was out of love that I went there."

"Then why don't you tell him?"

"Tell me what?" Nick asked.

"Don't listen to him. He twists words into lies," Theo said.

"Tell him who his real father is, Theo. Why he's the prince."

Nick looked in panic at Theo. "What is he talking about?"

"He's talking nonsense." And then, with an anger Nick had never seen on Theo's face, he flew like a wild bird through the air and struck the monk, who was sent reeling backward.

"Give me the sand!" the monk said.

Theo screamed out, "Nick, dump the sand. It doesn't mean anything. The family is everything."

Nick looked around the desert scene. Isabella was still lying on the ground, unconscious, with Irina tending to her. Damian looked like he was bleeding. It was only Nick and Theo against the monk.

"Dump the sand, Nick!" Theo commanded. "He will not get what he came here for. Not as long as we are united."

Nick pulled his sword and sent the gleaming blade across the desert sky. It struck the monk's face, drawing blood. Nick gasped. It was exactly as Boris had told him—the sword, used rightly, would find its mark.

"Dump the sand, Nick!" Theo urged.

Nick hesitated.

"Nick…for once, you have to trust me."

Nick nodded. Though he knew his mother had died to

protect the sand, he opened his palm, and the golden flecks floated away on a morning breeze.

"Noooooo!" screamed the monk as blood dripped from the slash on his face.

"That cut is for Boris!" Nick screamed. He took the pouch and upturned it, sending the rest of the sand scattering. It was caught up in a gust, and he watched the gold flecks flying through the air.

Theo then waved his hands and spun around, pulling the sands up into a swirling sandstorm cloud. The sand spun, faster and faster, like a tornado's funnel cloud, and then Theo sent it directly at the monk. The sandstorm picked up the Shadowkeeper, pulling him into the swirling mass and sweeping him away, toward the desert's far horizon. Nick could hear the monk's anguished cry, carried like an echo across the desert.

Nick watched as Theo's face was consumed by concentration, until he finally fell to the ground, exhausted, the sandstorm nothing more than a speck in the distance.

Nick knelt by Theo's side. "Are you okay?"

"I am if you are."

Nick nodded. Then he ran to Isabella's side. "Wake up, favorite cousin. Wake up."

Her eyes fluttered.

Nick hugged her. "You're okay!"

She nodded, her face still pale, her lips dry and chapped. "Nick?"

"Yeah?"

"Before we go back home…can I try a piece of pizza?"

Nick threw his head back and laughed. "Pizza and cheeseburgers. I don't care what anyone else says."

NO GOING BACK

AMIAN STRUGGLED TO STAND, AND NICK AND THEO WENT
to his side to support him. "Look, over there," Damian
pointed.

The Eternal Hourglass stood, upside down, in a sand drift.

"He must have dropped it when Theo sent him flying."

The five of them limped toward the hourglass. Damian
frowned. "I'm glad he didn't get it, but it's one of our relics.
Lost forever."

"Maybe not," Nick said, smiling.

"What do you mean?"

Nick pulled out a pouch from his other pocket. "This is
the sand."

"What?" Theo asked incredulously. "What was that sand
you poured into the desert?"

Nick grinned. "Desert sand. I scooped some up. What traveled on the wind was just sand. Not Eternal Hourglass sand. In the end, the mighty Rasputin was fooled by a simple sleight of hand."

Damian laughed and ruffled his hair. "Genius, cousin! Genius! A trick worthy of the family. Worthy of your rightful place among us."

"Can we go home now?" Nick asked.

"And can we get pizza?" Isabella asked.

"Both," said Damian. He walked unsteadily over to Maslow and patted the horse. "He was a wise choice, don't you think?"

Nick nodded.

Damian stared at him. He didn't say anything, but for Nick, the gaze was enough.

"We better fly. We have a show tonight."

Inwardly, Nick groaned. But he realized now that was Damian's way. It was about the show, which united them all together. And the show must go on.

✧ ✧ ✧

"Here you go, Grand Duchess," Nick whispered.

After Damian had magically transported them home, and after they'd had the promised pizza, taken showers, watered Maslow, and recovered from their injuries, Nick brought the now magically repaired Eternal Hourglass up to the Grand Duchess's room and set it gently in her lap.

She ran her crooked, ancient fingers around its rim, pressing on the Cyrillic lettering. "It's true, you know."

"What is?"

"Time stands still for no man. I sometimes wish for the days of my youth. The days before the evil that was the monk. The days of the Little Pair and the Big Pair. Grief lessens with time, but it still seems to ignore time, to feel as fresh sometimes as a knife wound."

"But we have this relic back now, Grand Duchess. It's ours again."

She nodded. "But he lives."

"Maybe he will stay away. Go hunting other relics."

"Maybe. I think *you*, my young Kolya, are the relic he desires most."

"Me?"

"You are a Gazer. One born to each generation."

"So Damian...and now me?"

She smiled enigmatically. "Theo and now you."

She lifted up her heavy crystal candy dish. "Sweet?"

"No, thank you." Nick looked out at the snow falling on the casino. The newspapers and television had declared the new show to be the biggest success in the history of Las Vegas. He was being hailed as a daredevil, as a new magician in his own right. The incident with Maslow running loose on the Las Vegas Strip was cleverly "spun" by a casino spokesperson—his third cousin Dmitri—as merely a publicity stunt.

"Grand Duchess?" Nick asked.

"Yes, dear?"

"Can I ask you something?"

"Certainly."

"What did Rasputin mean? When he told Theo to tell me the truth about being the prince? What else is the family hiding from me?"

The Grand Duchess pulled a diamond comb from her chignon—five gems the size of dimes across it—and repositioned it in her snow-white hair.

"I cannot tell you that, Nicholai. There are secrets those two brothers keep. I can only tell you that after your mother died, they changed."

"How?"

"Theo stopped performing."

"He used to perform?"

"They were an act. The two of them together. An act that—perhaps until last night—had never been equaled anywhere in the world. But after that, Theo devoted himself to family history, to the legacy, to relic hunting, to teaching. He's buried in books and history, never resting, never sleeping. I think, all these years, Theo has been waiting for you."

"But in the desert, he was stronger than Damian."

"Come closer. I have a secret."

Nick leaned in. The Grand Duchess leaned close to him, and in a ghostly whisper said, "You are stronger than both of them. You just need to find your destiny."

Nick nodded and stared out at the snow. He worried about the family, about the monk coming back. Now he knew why the Grand Duchess spent her time pondering the snow. It was the responsibility weighing on her. He felt the weight of the family on his own shoulders.

He wished he had never seen a Shadowkeeper. The vision still came to him sometimes. Their faces melting into black oil, sprouting wings, their agony. He didn't want that vision in his brain. He didn't want any visions. He wished he was still back in his room at the Pendragon, which seemed so long ago. She was right. Time didn't stand still.

His destiny, like time, marched on.

And like releasing the sand, there was no going back.

A PRINCE RISES

ICK WALKED INTO THE CLASSROOM. THEO WAS WRITING in a massive book with a fountain pen filled with magic invisible ink. Nick knew it was the only kind he used.

"What's that?"

With a flourish, Theo wrote the last letter in what Nick guessed was Cyrillic and then shut the book.

"Family history. I continue recording each event, every birth, every death, every cataclysmic event, every relic found, every battle, every secret. You are now part of *history*. You helped defeat Rasputin…this time."

"What did he mean about the truth, Theo?"

Theo shook his head. "What is truth?"

"You speak in riddles. Everyone does."

"Maybe that's the family way."

"But why doesn't everyone just come out with it?"

He laughed. "Maybe that's the Russian way. You know, Russians, for centuries, were known for one trait: brooding. I used to wonder why. Now, I think it's all about this." He patted the book.

"There you go again. What are you talking about?"

"The history of our family is tied to the history of Mother Russia. It's not a happy history. The more you learn of her, the more you will understand why the Grand Duchess stares out at the snow all day long." He knocked on his desk three times then spat over his shoulder three times. "We speak no more of dark things. Only good."

Nick sighed. Obviously, he wasn't going to get any more answers today.

"I need to go get ready for the show."

"One more thing." Theo stood, walked over to Nick, and handed him a book. "Don't tell Damian. And use it wisely."

Nick looked down and opened the cover. The pages were blank, but at his touch, they filled in with Cyrillic. And then a name appeared on the inside front cover. *Tatyana*. "This is my mother's book of spells."

"Remember…like your sword, the crystal, all magic, abuse it and you will find that the truth is even more difficult to ascertain."

Nick nodded and walked out of the classroom, down to his own room. Once inside, he set the book down next to the imperial eggs. He wanted to find out more about what happened to his mother. But maybe Theo was right. Maybe truth wasn't as easy to find as he thought.

Nick lay down on his bed, and before he knew it, he was sound asleep.

✫　✫　✫

Nick woke up with a seven-hundred-pound tiger on his chest, smelling the fishy breath of Sascha and feeling the tiger's whiskers tickling his cheek.

"Get up!" Isabella screamed at him. She was standing next to his bed, already in her costume. "We're due to go on in twenty minutes. If you're late, Damian will kill you."

"If you would kindly get your tiger off my chest…"

Sascha didn't move until Isabella snapped her fingers. Sometimes, that tiger could be so infuriating.

Nick leaped from bed, hurriedly pulled one of his costumes from the closet, and started putting the shirt on. "Let's go!"

They ran down the hall, Sascha bounding beside them, as Nick buttoned his shirt, the jeweled collar scratching his neck slightly.

From beneath the bowels of the casino, they raced along concrete hallways and emerged in the full bustle of the largest show in Las Vegas and perhaps the world.

For the briefest of moments, Nick stood still, as his cousins and aunts and uncles and distant relatives, as the whole family ran around him, "Places! Come on!"

He could hear the violins tuning in the orchestra pit.

His cousin Olga walked up to him, adjusted his collar, and ran a comb through his hair.

Damian spied him and charged at him, fury on his face. "Get in the tunnel. Now! Get to Maslow! And don't ever be late again!"

Nick looked at Isabella.

"Remember, no mess!" she joked.

In one wing off the stage, Irina rehearsed with the polar bears.

Theo nodded and waved from the other wing.

Smiling, Nick rode down a small lift to a dimly lit tunnel. Ahead of him, he could hear his beloved horse whinnying for him. Behind him was his family, his destiny stretching back through centuries and forward toward his future.

He ran, his boots echoing on the metal, reached Maslow, and climbed on his back. "You did good out there in the desert, my friend," he whispered.

The horse lifted his head majestically, as befitting an Akhal-Teke.

The orchestra began.

Boom-boom-boom went the timpani.

The trapdoor opened, and Nicholai Rostov and his horse were lifted up out of the casino's basement into the spotlight.

Nick sat high on his horse. He lifted his head. He let the spotlight gleam on him.

As befitting a prince of the Magickeepers.

The adventure continues in Book Two of
the Magickeepers series

PROLOGUE

Spring Garden district, Philadelphia, 1844

*E*DGAR ALLAN POE SAT AT HIS WOODEN DESK AND STARED out the window at the midnight sky. His wife, Virginia, was in the small back bedroom, coughing in her sleep. Tuberculosis was ravaging her health, and Poe was even more desperate now for a hit. A poem or short story that would capture the imagination of an editor and the nation and make him wealthy, famous, and able to care for her.

But inspiration did not come.

He stared down at the paper, quill pen in his hand.

But all he saw was a white page taunting him with its blankness. No words came to him.

He took a sip of dark red brandy. More than he cared to admit, that was often where he got his inspiration. But tonight, the muse did not come.

"Please," he whispered desperately, almost a prayer. "Inspiration. That is what I need."

From the back bedroom, he heard Virginia's rattling cough.

He put his head in his hands, anguish etched across his pale face.

"Tat-tat-tat."

Poe jumped near out of his skin at the sound. He stared at the brandy bottle. Was he now having hallucinations?

But then he heard the sound again.

Something was at the window.

Yet that was impossible. He was on the second floor.

Shaking, he stood and crept toward the panes of glass, peering out into the darkness.

"Tat-tat!"

A more insistent sound. The pecking of a beak at the window.

Squinting in the lamplight, Poe cautiously opened the window. A large black bird stared at him inquisitively from the sill. Blinking twice, it stepped across the sill and alighted on the floor.

"Once upon a midnight dreary," the bird spoke in a voice as clear as Poe's own.

Poe took three steps backward and fell into a chair.

"I *am* hallucinating," he muttered to himself.

"Nothing of the sort. I am here to bring you your deepest desire."

"A raven . . . to answer my deepest desire? How do you propose that?" Poe said, scarce believing he was talking to a bird, still half-certain it was all a dream or a bad batch of brandy.

"My name is Miranda. I have come as an answer to your prayer. Write down what I say, and you will be rewarded."

Poe stared at the bird.

"Your pen. Begin writing," the bird insisted. She took several hops and preened her feathers, which shone like mica in the lamplight.

Poe returned to his desk, still not certain of anything—including his own sanity. He dipped his quill in ink and began copying down the raven's words.

"While I nodded, nearly napping . . ." the bird spoke.

And Poe scribbled.

When the bird was finally done speaking, Poe stared down at eighteen stanzas of poetry, six lines each. It was perfection. The greatest poem he had ever written. Even if they weren't his words.

"That poem shall make you famous, Edgar Allan Poe," the raven said proudly. She stretched her wings and shook her tail feathers.

"But why have you come to me?" Poe asked, staring down at the poem, and still marveling at its perfection.

Miranda flew and landed on his desk, her eyes shone like two black diamonds of many facets.

"In exchange for this poem, someday I shall return to you and ask you for a favor. You may not refuse me, Edgar Allan Poe, or you will experience ruin and death. Is that understood?"

"But what kind of favor?" Poe asked.

"A magical favor. I may need for you to hold something for me, for safekeeping. From forces you cannot understand. Shadows."

Poe swallowed. Could this bargain be worth it? But there, staring at him, were the words on the paper, so magnificent. They were worth anything. Surely they were.

He nodded at the bird. "We have a deal."

"Excellent," spoke the raven. Outside a fierce wind rose up from nowhere, filling the room with an icy chill. "They are near," the bird whispered. She took flight and soared out the window, her call echoing through the night. "They are near! They are near!"

Edgar Allan Poe ran to the window and shut it, locking it, in fear for his life.

He returned to his desk, sweating nervously despite the cold air. What kind of deal had he just made, he wondered?

And what would it cost him?

ABOUT THE AUTHOR

Erica Kirov is an American writer of Russian descent. Though she is not from a family of magicians, she is from a proud family of Russians, and she grew up hearing stories of their lives there.

Erica lives in Virginia with her husband, four children, three dogs, parrot, hedgehog, and her son's snake (she really hates snakes). She is busy at work on the next Magickeepers novel, and you can read more about the Magickeepers at www.magickeepers.com.